Brief ENCOUNTERS

NATSUME SŌSEKI

Natsume Sōseki (1867–1916) is considered one of Japan's greatest and most influential modern writers. Born to a wealthy, landowning family who put him up for adoption, Sōseki was marked by childhood insecurities, further compounded by the death of his mother. Much against the wishes of his family, he dreamt of a life as a writer, and after a career in teaching, including several years in London, he embarked on his literary career in 1903. The success of *I Am a Cat*, first serialised in 1905, brought Sōseki nationwide fame, and he went on to write some of Japan's most cherished contemporary novels, including *Kokoro*, *Botchan* and *Kusamakura*.

NATSUME SŌSEKI

AN UNDESIRABLE FRIEND

Translated from the Japanese by
Nick Bradley

Brief ENCOUNTERS

VINTAGE CLASSICS

1 3 5 7 9 10 8 6 4 2

Vintage Classics is part of the Penguin Random House group of companies

Vintage, Penguin Random House UK, One Embassy Gardens,
8 Viaduct Gardens, London SW11 7BW

penguin.co.uk/vintage-classics
global.penguinrandomhouse.com

This edition published in Vintage Classics in 2026
First published in *I Am a Cat* by Vintage Classics in 2025

Translation copyright © Nick Bradley 2025

The moral right of the translator has been asserted

Typeset in 13.4/16pt Bembo Book MT Pro by Six Red Marbles UK, Thetford, Norfolk
Printed and bound in Great Britain by Clays Ltd, Elcograf S.p.A.

The authorised representative in the EEA is Penguin Random House Ireland,
Morrison Chambers, 32 Nassau Street, Dublin D02 YH68

A CIP catalogue record for this book is available from the British Library

ISBN 9781529983654

Penguin Random House is committed to a sustainable future
for our business, our readers and our planet. This book is made
from Forest Stewardship Council® certified paper.

It seems that I've become a little famous this New Year; being a cat – and above all that nonsense – I'm grateful I can carry on holding my head high with pride.

Early on New Year's Day, a picture postcard arrived for the master. It was a simple nengajo New Year's greeting card from a painter friend of his, but the top part was painted red, the bottom a dark green, and in the middle was some kind of animal squatting in a formal sumo pose, drawn in pastels. The master was examining it from all angles in his study, turning it from side to side repeatedly, alternating between portrait and landscape, all the while saying, 'Wonderful colours!'

He'd shown quite enough admiration for it already, and I thought he was about to give it a rest, but he started gazing at it once more, continually rotating it between portrait and landscape. He began to contort and twist his body in order to look at it better, he held it at arm's length as though he were a wise man reading an ancient text, then he tilted it towards the light of the window and put the card right up close to his nose. I was trying to get comfortable on his lap, and so I sincerely hoped he would put an end to all this kerfuffle soon, because his knees kept wobbling as he jostled me. And just when I thought all the commotion was calming itself, he said in a very small voice, 'What on earth has he drawn here?'

I had been mistaken all this time – while the master had indeed admired the colour of the card, he had no idea what animal was drawn in its centre. That's what all his fussing had been about. Thinking it was only an incomprehensible picture postcard, I elegantly half-opened my sleepy eyes, and calmly took a better look for myself. There was no mistaking the fact. It was a portrait of me. While experts such as Andrea del Sarto or my master, with his, *ahem*, 'refined' tastes, might not deem it a masterpiece, the perfectly captured colour and shape were what one would expect from a professional painter. Anyone could tell that the thing being represented in the drawing was undoubtedly a cat. Honestly, I'd go further to say, it was so beautifully drawn that anyone with an ounce of discernment could clearly see it was a perfect depiction of *yours truly* – not just any old mog. For a man to go to such pains to look at a picture, and still not see something so obvious . . . well, I pity the human race. If I were able to, I would've liked to set him straight and tell him the drawing was of none other than myself. Gosh, even if I couldn't convey to the numbskull that it was me, I'd at least have liked to make him understand that it was a drawing of a cat. Humans are a lowly animal, however, not blessed with the heavenly gift of comprehending our ancient and refined cat language. So, whilst it was a huge shame, I let the matter be.

But, ladies and gentlemen, this brings me on to something I'd like to impress upon you, and make an appeal to your better nature. This recent tendency humans have to look down on us cats and say things with casual contempt like, '*bloody cats!*' . . . it's not good, I tell you. It's common for people – let's even say, teachers – who are puffed up with arrogance and ignorant of their own stupidity, to think things like, '*The gods made cows and horses from human leftovers, and then from the turds of cows and horses, they made cats.*' Now, whichever way you look at it, these aren't the thoughts or words of a dignified or educated person, are they? It's absurd. A cat couldn't have been made in such a crude, simple way. If one were to line up a row of cats, the untrained eye might start by saying they were equally indiscriminate, lacking any defining idiosyncrasies. However, if they were to look again more closely and truly enter Cat Society, things become more complicated. It's like the old human proverb:

十人十色 Ten people, ten colours

Everyone is different – and this is equally true for cats. The eyes, the nose, the fur, the paws – they all vary drastically. From the springiness of the whiskers to the manner in which they prick up their ears, even down to the hang of the tail, no two cats are ever the same. We have infinitely varied personalities, too – nimble, clumsy, stylish, vulgar, our own specific likes and dislikes – the list is endless. In spite of the fact that we have such clear distinctions, the human eye, ever in search of what they call 'progress and advancement', is constantly staring at the sky, so it's no wonder they can't tell our looks and features apart, let alone our personalities – and what a shame. But like another old proverb says: *birds of a feather flock together*. If I want the tastiest mochi rice cake I'll buy it from the mochi shop, and likewise, if I want to hear anything interesting or insightful about cats, I'll go ask a cat directly, thank you very much. Humans, for all their lofty talk and pride in their own 'progress and advancement' know nothing about cats. The cold hard truth of all this is, humans are not even a whisker as wonderful as they believe themselves to be.

Take my master, for example, a man of such meagre compassion he fails to grasp that mutual understanding is the primary requisite of love – what hope is there for such a man as him? Like an ill-natured oyster, he fastens himself to a cushion in his study, without so much as a care for who does what out there in the world. Instead, he sits by himself with an ever-so-wise and philosophical expression on his face – it's hilarious.

Currently, the proof that he lacks a single scrap of wisdom was lying right under his nose in the form of my portrait – which he still couldn't decipher, but instead burbled utter nonsense like, 'Hmm . . . I suppose . . . well now, as this year marks the second year of the Russo-Japanese war . . . perhaps . . . perhaps it could be a Russian bear . . .?'

I was resting my eyes, snoozing on my master's lap and thinking deeply about all of this, when before long the maidservant brought in a *second* picture postcard. When I looked at it I saw it was a print depicting four or five cats of Western breeds, all sitting in a row. Some were reading books, some holding pens, and they looked to be studying. One of the cats had left its seat, and was dancing some crazy cat jig up on the table. Above the scene, someone had written in jet-black sumi ink with a Japanese brush, 'I, ladies and gentlemen, am a cat.' On the right-hand side of the card was a haiku, written in the same hand:

書を読むや
踊るや猫の
春一日

One could read a book,

Or dance, dance like a mad cat!

On a fine spring day.

This was from my master's former pupil, and anyone need only take a single glance at it to work out what it meant, yet the ninny still hadn't clocked what all the cat stuff was about, and was currently cocking his head to one side in puzzlement, muttering to himself, 'Is it the Year of the Cat . . .?' His mind must be addled. Everyone knows the cat isn't even one of the twelve animals of the zodiac.

Apparently, he still had absolutely no idea just how famous I'd become.

Shortly thereafter the maidservant brought in a third card. This one did not have a picture, just a written message:

Happy New Year.
P.S. Please convey my heartfelt wishes to your little cat, too.

On reading this, even my useless master could finally comprehend what was going on. Realization dawning, he looked my way, raised an eyebrow and let out a single, 'Hmm.' In his gaze I thought I could detect a newfound respect, and rightly so – up until that point he had been an utter nobody, and it was only thanks to me that he was starting to gain a name in society, so I think it only fair he give me the acclaim I deserve.

Just then, the bell at the gate gave a little *tinkle tinkle*. A visitor, most likely, and the maidservant went to deal with the matter. I have a policy of not greeting visitors (unless it happens to be Umeko-san the fishmonger). And so, I remained calmly curled up on my master's lap. The master, meanwhile, pulled a pained expression and eyed the genkan entranceway nervously. He obviously found the idea of having to receive New Year's callers and drink saké with them unbearably disagreeable. There really is no hope for such a human who has become so warped and eccentric. If he really doesn't want to accept visitors, he should've got up early and left the house, but he doesn't even have the courage to do that. As I mentioned, he's becoming more like an oyster with every passing day.

Presently, the maidservant returned, bringing with her Kangetsu-kun. This Kangetsu fellow happens to be another one of the master's former pupils. However, as the age-old story goes, Kangetsu-kun has attained a good position in society since graduating and is now doing far, far better than his former teacher. Yet, for some reason or other, this chap keeps coming to pay his respects to the master. And whenever he comes, he brings with him spicy gossip pertaining to his adventures in society: tales of women who love him, and women who don't; stories of how he's been enjoying life in the big wide world, and how he sometimes finds society dull. Why on earth he comes all this way to regale a shrivelling old fart like my master, I simply have no idea, but it's amusing to watch the oyster listening, all the while nodding his oyster-like head, and even sometimes chiming in with his oyster-ish opinions.

'Apologies for not calling in a while. The truth is, I was so busy in the lead-up to the New Year that whenever I thought to myself, *Come on! Let's go out!* my feet just wouldn't point in this direction,' said Kangetsu-kun cryptically, all the while fiddling with the string of his haori overcoat.

'I wonder which way they ended up pointing,' said the master with a serious expression on his face, pulling up the cuffs of his own black cotton haori jacket, emblazoned with the family crest. This cotton haori overcoat was far too short in the seams, so much so that his old worn-out kimono protruded from underneath, a couple of inches on both his left and his right.

'*Eh heh heh . . .* they definitely ended up pointing in the wrong direction,' said Kangetsu-kun, laughing.

I could see now that Kangetsu was missing a front tooth.

'Good God! What happened to your tooth, man?' asked the master, changing the subject.

'Erm, I went to eat some shiitake mushrooms at a certain establishment –'

'What's that you said you ate?'

'Erm, shiitake mushrooms. Well, when I tried to take a bite out of a mushroom cap . . . my tooth broke off.'

'Losing your tooth to a mushroom makes you sound like an old codger. Good for a haiku maybe, but it's hardly going to bring the women running,' said the master, lightly patting my head as he spoke.

'Ah! So that's the famous cat. Looks to be quite stout, no? I'd say he'd give the rickshaw man's cat, Mr Kuro, a run for his money. He's a handsome fellow,' said Kangetsu-kun, lavishing me with praise.

'He's grown quite a bit recently,' boasted the master, patting my head again warmly.

I'd take all the praise coming, but my head was beginning to pound from all this patting.

'The other night we put on another little recital,' said Kangetsu-kun, returning to their conversation.

'Where?'

'*Where* doesn't matter – you've missed it already. We had three violins and a piano for accompaniment. It was pretty good – even if the players aren't great, as long as you have at least three violins it's easy on the ears. There were two young lady violinists, and me in the middle between them. I thought I played rather well.'

'Hmm . . . and who were these two young ladies?' asked the master with palpable envy.

Despite my master's usual withered and stony countenance, he's by no means apathetic or indifferent towards the fairer sex. One time, he was reading a Western novel in which it was pointed out to a male character that he fell in love with almost every woman he met, another character having totted up the numbers in jest. It was calculated that he fell for 70 per cent of all the women he crossed paths with. This seemed entirely factual to the master and made a deep impression on him. As a humble cat, I have no idea why someone who has made the decision to live the life of an oyster found this capricious character from a novel so fascinating. Perhaps he wants to be like him, in which case what on earth is stopping him? There's talk that the master had his heart broken in the past – or it could be his weak stomach, or the fact he has no money, or maybe just his cowardly make-up in general. Whatever it is, one thing is for sure: when the history books of the Meiji Period are written, you won't find the master mentioned on any of their pages, so ultimately it really makes no difference. However, I could tell from the way he asked Kangetsu-kun about the women that he was obviously envious.

Kangetsu-kun picked at a side dish of baked fish paste with his chopsticks and took a bite with his missing front tooth. I was worried he'd lose another, but he was all right this time.

'Oh, just two ladies of well-to-do families. I'm sure you don't know them,' he answered perfunctorily.

'Oh, I . . .' The master trailed off, presumably omitting the word 'see' (which he must've said in his head).

By this time, Kangetsu-kun had apparently had
enough of the master's laziness.

'The weather is wonderful today. If you're not too
busy and have nothing better to do, how about going
out for a stroll? Our victory at Port Arthur over the
Russians has put everyone in high spirits – the town
is all a-bustle. It really is quite something.'

The master, who from his expression clearly
wanted to hear less about Port Arthur and more
about the ladies, was quiet for a while before making
a decision.

'All right, let's go out.' He stood up resolutely.

Under his crested black cotton haori overcoat he
wore a kimono made from silk that was produced in
a town, Yuki, in Ibaraki prefecture. The kimono had
been given to him by his older brother some twenty
years ago. Now, no matter how sturdy they say Yuki
silk is, if worn the way the master wears it, it is not
indestructible. His particular garment, when held up
to the light, instantly revealed threadbare patches of
stitching here and there. He wore the same thing all
year round, day in day out. Whatever the occasion.
Even when leaving the house, he'd just shove his
hands into his sleeves and go out like that. Whether he
had other clothes, or simply couldn't be bothered to
change them, I have no idea. But this sartorial neglect
can't be entirely down to his bad luck in love – or at
least, I don't think so.

After they'd both left, I took the liberty of pilfering the remaining half of Kangetsu-kun's baked fish paste, which he'd bitten into earlier. Now, ladies and gentlemen, recently I've come to the realization that I am no ordinary cat. First of all, I'd hazard I'm a finer cat than any mentioned in the famous rakugo storyteller Momokawa Joen's *Tales of a Hundred Cats*, or even the beloved cat of the eighteenth-century English poet Thomas Gray's immortal verse, a cat whose efforts to catch goldfish inspired Gray's 'Ode on the Death of a Favourite Cat Drowned in a Tub of Goldfishes'. And you can forget about cats like the rickshaw man's Mr Kuro. No one can begrudge me half a stick of baked fish paste. Besides, it's not just cats who have the bad habit of sneaking snacks between meals.

The kitchen maid, for example, often waits for the mistress to go out on errands before she raids the mochi, which she pinches and plunders, steals and scoffs. And it's not just the kitchen maid. The children — ever praised by the mistress for how elegantly she's brought them up — are at it, too, whenever backs are turned. Four or five days ago, the two children woke at an ungodly hour, and while the master and mistress were sleeping, they sat down opposite one another at the dining table. Every morning they eat a portion of the master's bread, with a little bit of sugar sprinkled on top. The sugar pot had already been laid out on the table, with a spoon.

As no one was around to dish out the sugar as usual, the bigger child eventually took up the spoon and scooped out a spoonful on to her own plate. Then, the smaller child copied her older sister, and in the same manner scooped out a spoonful on to her own plate. Their eyes met and they glared at each other. The bigger child took hold of the spoon and piled another scoop of sugar on to her plate. The smaller one immediately grabbed the spoon and piled the same amount on to hers. Then, the older sister took another scoop. The younger sister, not wanting to be outdone, took another. The older sister put her hand on the jar, and the younger sister picked up the spoon. Under my watchful gaze, spoonful after spoonful became a mountain of sugar piled up high on each of their plates, until there wasn't a single speck left in the pot. At which point, the master emerged from the bedroom rubbing his sleepy eyes, and carefully poured both mountains of sugar back into the pot from whence they came.

Seeing all this, I arrived at the conclusion that while humans, in their quest for selfishness, may well be superior to cats in their sense of fairness, in wisdom they are much inferior. I thought to myself, *all the time the children wasted making those mountains of sugar would have been better spent licking up as much of it as they could.* However, as always, my words never get through to them, and so while it was a great shame to have missed an opportunity to lick up all that sugar, I merely watched silently from my favourite snoozing spot, curled up on the warm wooden rice pot.

Wherever it was that Kangetsu-kun and the master went for a walk, he didn't get home till late that evening, and didn't arrive at the breakfast table until nine o'clock the next day. From my vantage point on the wooden rice pot I watched the master silently eating New Year's mochi rice cake, served in a fish and vegetable soup. Chew and swallow, chomp and slurp. The slices of mochi were thin but he must have eaten at least six or seven pieces before finally putting his chopsticks down and saying, 'I've had enough,' leaving one piece in his bowl. If anyone else were to be as childish in their eating habits as that, believe me we'd never hear the end of it. But because the master takes satisfaction in running the household like a hypocritical little despot, he was completely fine with the terrible crime of leaving that single burnt piece of mochi uneaten, languishing like a corpse in the cloudy dregs of the soup. When his wife went to the cupboard, took out a bottle of milk of magnesia and placed it on the table next to him, he piped up immediately.

'That stuff doesn't do a thing, so I'm not taking it any more,' he said.

'But it's apparently very effective against starchy things like mochi, so it probably would be best if you could just partake of a little,' she said, trying to get him to swallow the stuff.

'Starch or whatever, I'm telling you it doesn't work.' He stubbornly stuck to his guns.

'You really are capricious . . .' she said, as if speaking to herself.

'It's got nothing to do with anyone being capricious – the medicine simply doesn't work!'

'But wait a minute, who was it who said just the other day, "*Wow this stuff really works!*" and was glugging it down daily?'

'It worked then. It doesn't work now,' he replied antithetically.

'If you keep taking it and then stopping, even the most effective medicine won't do anything. You need to be a little more patient – dyspepsia can't be cured as easily as other illnesses.' She turned to the kitchen maid, who was serving the family from a silver tray. 'Isn't that so?'

'Yes, that's true,' said the kitchen maid, immediately siding with the mistress. 'If you don't keep taking it and giving it a chance to work, you'll never know whether it's a good or bad medicine.'

'Doesn't matter, because I'm not touching the stuff any more. And what do you two women know anyway? Put a cork in it, the pair of you.'

'Yes, we're women. And what of it?' said the mistress, moving the milk of magnesia and positioning it directly in front of him as though placing a ceremonial dagger before him so that he might commit seppuku ritual suicide at the breakfast table.

The master stood without a word and retreated to his study. His wife and the maid looked at one another and grinned.

After these sorts of episodes, I know from hard-won experience that it's not the best idea to follow him and get up on his lap. And so, I went to the garden to stretch my legs, then padded up on to the engawa wooden veranda and took a peek through the gap in the paper sliding doors into the study. The master was looking at a book by the stoic philosopher Epictetus. If he was really taking in anything about stoicism right now, I would have been considerably impressed. But five or six minutes passed before he threw the book down on the desk, where it landed with a loud thud. Exactly as I thought. And then I observed him take out his diary and make the following entry:

Went for a walk with Kangetsu around the Nezu, Ueno, Ikenohata and Kanda neighbourhoods. At Ikenohata, we ran into a geisha dressed in a spring kimono with an intricate design on the skirt. She was playing badminton. Her clothes were stunning, but her face was really quite unattractive. Looked a bit like our cat, somehow.

Now, it seems slightly unfair of him to single me out as an archetypal example of an unattractive face. If I were to go to Kitadoko's barbershop down the road and have my face shaved, I wouldn't look so different to a human, now would I? The self-conceit of humans really bothers me.

When we turned the corner where Hotan the Chemist is, another geisha came along. She had perfectly proportioned, long and slender shoulders, a truly wonderful woman. She looked ever so elegant, wearing an understated light purple kimono. When she smiled she revealed her white teeth. 'Gen-chan, about last night . . . it was because I was so busy,' she said. However, when she spoke . . . her voice . . . well, honestly, she crowed like an old tramp, and it rather undid all the hard work of her sophisticated appearance, so much so that I couldn't even be bothered to turn my head to look at this Gen-chan she was talking to. I kept my hands tucked firmly into my sleeves and carried on in the direction of Onarimachi. Kangetsu appeared somewhat on edge.

There is nothing as difficult to understand as human psychology. Indeed, what was going on in the mind of the master right now as he was writing? Was he angry? Was he happy? Was he seeking comfort in the written teachings of a dead stoic philosopher? I have absolutely no idea. Was he sneering at society? Or did he long to immerse himself deeply within that very same society? Was he angry at a trivial matter? Or was he aloof and detached from all worldly things? It was pure conjecture on my part.

Cats, on the other hand, are simple and straight-forward beings. If we want to eat, we eat. If we want to sleep, we sleep. When we get angry, we're angry with every hair follicle on our bodies. When we cry, we cry our hearts out. In any case, we have absolutely no need of such a pointless thing as a diary. Why, we'd have nothing to write in it, for a start. For a duplicitous person like the master, who needs to write his two-faced ideas down in a diary and hide them all away from the world in a dark room, it's perhaps necessary, but not for all of us honest cats, no. We keep our diaries open to the whole world in all we do, whether it be walking, sitting, standing or lying down – even going so far as urinating (and defecating) in public. What would be the point in going to all that effort of keeping a diary, when with us, what you see is what you get. If I had the luxury of time to waste writing a diary, I'd rather put it to better use: napping on the wooden veranda.

Ate supper at a certain restaurant in Kanda. Had two or three cups of delicious Masamune brand saké, from Nada-ku in Kobe. It'd been a while since I'd drunk saké, but this morning my stomach felt very good. Think a cup or two with my evening meal might be the best remedy for my dyspepsia. Forget about that milk of magnesia rubbish. Whatever anyone says, it doesn't do a thing. Whichever way you spin it – something that doesn't have any effect, simply doesn't work.

Notice, here, how he randomly attacks milk of magnesia, apropos of nothing. It's almost as if he's having an argument with himself. The remnants of this morning's anger rears its ugly head once more. Perhaps it's at these telling junctures that a human diary reveals the true nature of human beings.

The other day ○○-san said that if one skipped breakfast one's stomach would improve, so for three or four days I didn't eat breakfast at all, but my stomach just rumbled and gurgled the whole time and it had no effect. △△-san advised me to cut out pickled things like tsukemono from my diet. According to his theory, all stomach problems are caused by pickles. His argument being that one need only eradicate tsukemono, and thereby extinguish the cause of the stomach trouble without a shadow of a doubt. And so for one whole week I didn't so much as touch a single pickle with my chopsticks, but in the end, as I saw no beneficial effect, I started eating them again. ✕ ✕ -san told me that abdominal massage was the only way to sort the problem. He said that just two or three sessions with an expert in the old Miyagawa style would completely cure any stomach ailment. He told me that the famous Confucian scholar Yasui Sokken swore by this particular style of massage. And that even the bold and courageous samurai Sakamoto Ryoma was in the habit of receiving this same treatment from time to time. And so I took myself swiftly off, all the way to Kaminegishi in Chiba prefecture, to see what all the fuss was about. However, the masseur was an absolute sadist who told me it wouldn't get any better unless he massaged me all the way to the bone marrow, and flipped my intestines over on themselves once or twice – he squashed me to a pulp with his vice-like fingers. Afterwards, my body felt like cotton and my mind like I'd slipped into a coma. Needless to say, feeling a little fed up, I gave up on that pretty quickly.

A-kun told me not to eat solid food. After that I tried subsisting entirely on milk for a day, but my stomach rumbled and growled all night like a storm, and I couldn't sleep a wink. B-san told me that if I practised breathing exercises using my diaphragm, it would set my organs moving and cause the stomach to heal naturally. I tried this a little as well, but it made me feel strangely anxious deep down inside. Moreover, when I did remember to do it, despite at first concentrating and dedicating myself to it wholeheartedly, after about five or six minutes I'd forget to do it and I'd stop. And when I tried not to forget, I'd find myself incapable of thinking about anything but my diaphragm – so much so that I couldn't focus on my reading or writing. My Art Critic friend Meitei-san caught me doing these breathing exercises once and made fun of me, saying, '*Look, man, you're not giving birth, are you? So you'd better stop that at once.*' Ever since then, I've given up completely. C-sensei told me that eating soba noodles would do wonders for my stomach, so I wolfed down as much as I could – both hot and cold – but it did absolutely nothing for my stomach (if anything, it made matters worse). Over the years I've tried so many different methods to cure my stomach problems but they've all come to nothing. But those three cups of Masamune saké I had last night with Kangetsu seem to have worked a charm. I've decided I'll have two or three cups every night from now on.

And this new resolution of his probably won't continue for long. The master's heart and mind flits from one thing to the other as quickly as my feline pupils react to light and dark. Whatever he does, he's a man sorely lacking in persistence. In spite of his worries about his stomach, as the above entry clearly shows, he tries to cultivate the appearance that he's some kind of stoic, grinning and bearing it. The other day, a certain scholar friend of his came to visit. This scholar put forward the argument that all of our current illnesses are, in a sense, none other than the direct result of both our own and our ancestors' sins and vices (manifested in ourselves). He appeared to have really done his research, his reasoning was sound, and it was a splendid argument – well organized and systematic. And while regrettable, a man like my master did not have the intellect, understanding or knowledge to make any kind of rebuttal or retort. However, it seemed that just because he himself suffered from stomach troubles, he felt honour-bound to publicly make a case for himself – perhaps so he could save face.

'Your theory is interesting . . . however, Thomas Carlyle had dyspepsia,' said the master, as though merely by sharing the same illness as Carlyle that made him cut from the same cloth (as irrelevant an utterance as ever there was).

'Carlyle may have had dyspepsia, but that doesn't make everyone with dyspepsia Carlyle,' replied his friend, conclusively. To which the master remained silent.

In this way, we can plainly see that despite the master's vanity, he does truly want to be rid of his dyspepsia, and his resolution to have saké with his evening meal represents just another farcical episode in his farcical life. If you think about it, probably the reason he ate so many mochi rice cakes with his New Year's soup was a direct result of the hangover he was suffering from due to the cups of Masamune saké he knocked back with Kangetsu the night before.

On that note, I thought it high time I partook of some of that New Year's soup and mochi myself. Although I am a cat, I do eat ordinary food. I don't have the energy, like the rickshaw man's cat Mr Kuro, to go all the way on missions to raid the fish shop down the alleyway. And it goes without saying that I don't have the social standing to live in the lap of luxury like Miss Calico who lives with the koto teacher on the new road. So, contrary to what one might expect, I am not a fussy eater. I'll eat the crumbs of the children's leftover bread, I'll even lick up the sweet bean paste from a discarded mochi rice cake. Pickles aren't the most pleasant taste, but I've been known to eat a couple of slices of pickled daikon radish just to be able to say that I'd tried it. Most things I try, I find are edible. As a humble teacher's cat, I don't have the luxury of being so extravagant and fussy as to go about saying, 'I don't like this!' or 'I don't like that!'

According to my master there once was a French novelist named Balzac. This man was extremely over the top and extravagant – not in terms of what he ate, but in the way he went about writing his novels. One day when Balzac was working on a book, he'd been trying to come up with a name for a character, but couldn't hit upon one he liked. Shortly thereafter, a friend paid a visit, and they both went out for a stroll together. The friend had been dragged out unwittingly so that Balzac could continue on his quest to find the perfect name, walking wordlessly about town, doing nothing but looking at names on shop signs. Yet he still could not find one he liked. He continued dragging his friend along thoughtlessly and without explanation. The friend, without the faintest idea of what was going on, followed behind. The two of them tramped the streets of Paris from morning until nightfall. Then, when they were finally on their way home, Balzac suddenly noticed the sign of a tailor's shop. On it was written the name MARCUS. Balzac clapped his hands in glee.

'That's it! That's it! It has to be this! Isn't Marcus a great name? I'll add the initial Z, and then it's simply perfect. Without a Z it just won't do . . . *Z Marcus* – really has a nice ring to it. The name I had before was all right but felt a little contrived. Now I've finally got a name I'm pleased with,' he said, absolutely delighted with himself, but completely disregarding the trouble he had caused his friend.

To have to traipse the streets of Paris before naming each individual character in a novel seems a bothersome extravagance of the highest order. Which is all well and good for an over-the-top person like Balzac, but for a humble cat like myself, with an oysterish school teacher for a master – well, it's just not for me. The fact that I'll eat anything and I'm not particular about food is entirely down to my circumstances alone. So, it wasn't extravagance that now led me to want to eat some New Year's soup, but rather because I must eat whatever I can, whenever I can get my paws on it, and also, because I had just remembered that leftover piece of mochi in my master's soup he'd abandoned in the kitchen . . . And so, to the kitchen I went – just to have a look around, of course.

That same piece of mochi I'd seen that very morning was still as I'd seen it last; the same colour, adhering stickily to the bottom of the wooden bowl. Now, ladies and gentlemen, I have a confession to make. Up until that point in my life, I'd never tried that sticky rice-cake thing humans call 'mochi'. While it did indeed look delicious, something felt a little unsettling about the way it lay there. I dipped my front paw into the remaining soup and pulled the leafy greens out of the way. Prodding the surface of the mochi with a claw, I couldn't help noticing its gluey texture.

Upon giving it a tentative sniff, I was reminded a little of that particular aroma given off when the stuff at the bottom of the rice pot is scraped up and transferred to a bowl. Should I eat it, or should I give it a miss? I looked around nervously at the door. For better or for worse, I was alone. The kitchen maid was doing what she always does, playing badminton outside (whatever the season) with that same goofy look on her face. The children were in the living room singing a song called 'What Does the Rabbit Say?' If I was going to eat this mochi thing, now was the time. If I missed my chance, I'd have to spend another year without knowing the taste of mochi. Although I am just a humble cat, I perceived at this moment a singular universal truth:

A rare opportunity can often put an animal into an unfavourable situation.

If I'm being completely honest with myself, I didn't truly *want* to eat the mochi that much. In fact, the more I stared at it, stuck to the bottom of the wooden bowl, the less appealing it became. At that time, if the kitchen maid had opened the back door, or if I'd heard the pitter-patter of the children's feet heading this way, I would have ungrudgingly left the wooden bowl alone, and I can honestly say any curiosity about the taste of mochi wouldn't have bothered me for another year. However, no one came – no matter how much I hesitated – no one came. I began to feel a nagging voice in my head saying, *Aren't you gonna eat it? Aren't you gonna eat it soon?* Peering into the bowl again, I prayed that someone might come quickly. All the same, still no one did. I realized then that I was going to *have to* eat the mochi. At long last, I stuck my whole face and shoulders into the bowl and took a little bite. I calculated that at my usual bite strength I would nip clean through the stuff, and when I didn't, I was shocked! I thought to myself, *okay, that'll do*, but when I tried to pull my teeth apart they simply wouldn't move. I attempted another bite, to see if that might fix things, but my jaw wouldn't budge. By the time I'd realized that mochi was the devil's food, it was already far too late. Like a man stuck in a bog who sinks deeper by impatiently trying to get his legs free, my mouth became heavier the more I chewed, and my teeth wouldn't move. My teeth were the only answer I had to a problem caused by those very same teeth. Quite the paradoxical conundrum. The art critic, Meitei-sensei, once said of my master, 'You really are just an impossibly stubborn man!' and now I fully understood his meaning. The master and the mochi are both as impossibly stubborn as each other. No matter how much I chewed, even if I persevered until the end of time, I'd never get the better of this substance. It was while enduring this agony that I came upon a second universal truth:

All animals intuitively foresee what is good for them, and what is not.

Despite coming up with two very clever universal truths, I couldn't enjoy any sense of satisfaction at my cleverness because my mouth was glued shut by the infernal mochi. My teeth were being sucked into the mochi with such a force that I thought they might be yanked clean out. If I didn't get a move on and eat this cursed mochi, the kitchen maid would come back. The children's song had finished and there was no doubt they would come galloping into the kitchen at any moment. In desperation, I tried to thrash my tail about, and to prick my ears up in alarm, and then flatten them as low as they would go, but all to no avail. When I thought about it, my tail and ears really had absolutely nothing to do with the mochi. In short, I'd wasted precious tail and ear energy that could've been put to better use, so I stopped all that nonsense. Eventually, I came up with a genius plan to enlist the help of my two front paws in somehow scraping off the mochi. First, I used the right paw to stroke the outline of my mouth. But, there was no way that stroking was going to get me anywhere. Next, I extended my left paw, and devised a central role for it, swiping drastic, exaggerated circles aimed at my mouth. But even this action would not exorcise the demon. Patience is crucial, I thought to myself, and so I took turns trying with first the left paw, and then the right, but still my teeth became more firmly embedded in the mochi. Ugh, this was becoming really bothersome, and so I used both paws at once. Upon doing so, I realized that I was now miraculously walking on my two hind legs. It felt as though I was no longer a cat any more. Cat or not, either way, it didn't seem to matter much at this point. I was determined to go to any lengths – even clawing senselessly at my own face – until I was rid of the devilish mochi. I was waving my front paws so madly that I lost my sense of balance and began stumbling, in danger of toppling over. Unable to stand in one place, I was forced to jump madly around the kitchen, hopping from one paw to the other in order to prevent myself from falling over. Despite the severity of the situation, I thought myself pretty nimble in managing to stay upright, even if I do say so myself. A third universal truth appeared before my very eyes:

> In times of inordinate danger, the ordinarily impossible suddenly becomes extraordinarily possible. This is what's known as divine intervention.

And so, with the gift of this divine intervention, I waged war – tooth and claw – on the infernal mochi, when suddenly I heard the sound of footsteps approaching, and felt a burst of excitement that people were coming my way. But then, as it dawned on me how awful it would be to have someone come in when I was like this, I began to rush frantically around the kitchen in terror. The sound of footsteps drew ever nearer. Oh well . . . so much for my divine intervention.

It was the children who spotted me first.

'Oh wow! The cat ate some mochi and is doing a dance!' they shouted loudly.

The first person to hear the shout was the kitchen maid. She threw down her badminton racquet and shuttlecock, and barged inside.

'Oh my!' she said.

Then came the mistress in her silk kimono. 'Naughty cat!' she said.

Even the master emerged from his study and let out his customary, 'Stupid bastard!'

The children kept chanting, 'Look at him! It's hilarious!'

And then they all started guffawing in chorus, all in on the same joke, as if they'd rehearsed together beforehand. All the while, I was angry, in pain, tired, but I couldn't stop dancing. Eventually the laughter subsided, and the five-year-old said, 'Mother, that cat really is so silly!' This brought about another bout of roaring laughter.

I've observed a great deal when it comes to the matter of human beings and their complete lack of compassion, but this cruel occasion really took the biscuit. Finally, with divine intervention having completely deserted me, I went back to crawling on all fours, as is customary, my eyes black and white (spinning) and my mouth shut tight in shame and disgust. As expected, the master didn't want to see me die.

'Take the mochi out,' he ordered the kitchen maid.

She made eyes at the mistress as if to say, *Don't you want to make him dance some more?* It appeared that the mistress did, indeed, want to see me carry on dancing but didn't have it in her to murder me in cold blood, and so she remained silent.

'If you don't take it out soon, he'll die. Take it out now,' said the master once again to the maid.

As if she'd been woken from a dream in which she'd only been able to eat half a meal, the kitchen maid yanked the mochi from my mouth with a listless expression. My first thought was of Kangetsu, and that I might lose *all* my front teeth. Why did it hurt so much? Probably because of how mercilessly my firmly embedded teeth were wrenched from the mochi. It was then that I hit upon my fourth universal truth:

Comfort can only be reached by passing through great hardship.

I looked about myself, but everyone had gone to the living room.

Having made such a blunder, the last thing I wanted to do was hang about the house and awkwardly catch the kitchen maid's eye, or someone of her ilk. Rather, I decided I'd prefer a refreshing change of scenery and so I left the kitchen and took a stroll down the new road to pay Miss Calico a visit at the koto teacher's house – Miss Calico being a famous beauty in our neighbourhood.

Now, I may be a humble cat, but I'm a considerate cat, too, and know full well when my presence is unwanted. Whenever I see my master's face all puckered up and bitter, or when I don't feel like I can face a scolding from the kitchen maid, I'll invariably seek out the company of my female friend, and have a good old chat about all sorts of things. Upon doing so, before I know it, I feel my heart and mind fully refreshed, and I forget all my worries, concerns and worldly woes; I feel almost as if I've been reborn. The impact the fairer sex has on our lives and moods is truly colossal. I took a peep through the gap in the cedar fence, wondering to myself whether she was there or not, and then saw her sitting with perfect posture on the wooden veranda. As it was the New Year, she was sporting a brand-new collar. The curvature of her back was ineffably arresting. The very line of beauty itself. I cannot even begin to describe the charm of the scene: the graceful curve of her tail; the delicate fold of her paws; the sporadic, melancholic gentle movements of her ears.

She looked especially warm, sunbathing in a spot that caught the light perfectly. In her fine and elegant manner she appeared restrained, to say nothing of her silent and graceful demeanour. Her sleek and lustrous fur, which could be confused for pure velvet, reflected the New Year's sun in a way that made it quiver irresistibly as if blown by a soft breeze, and yet there was no wind to speak of. For a moment I gazed at the scene, entranced, but before long I came back to myself, and called out to her in a low voice.

'Miss Calico! Oh, Miss Calico!' I said, while beckoning her with my front paw.

'Oh! Professor! Is that you?' she said, coming down from the wooden veranda. The bell attached to her red collar jingled and jangled lightly. As she approached, I was thinking to myself what a lovely sound that bell made to bring in the New Year.

'Happy New Year, Professor!' she said, curling her tail slightly to the left.

When we cats greet one another, we stand our tails upright like poles and then lean them to the left. The only person in the neighbourhood who calls me 'Professor' is Miss Calico. As I've mentioned before, I still don't have a name. However, Miss Calico respectfully refers to me as *Professor* this, or *Professor* that owing to my living in the house of a teacher. As I find being referred to as professor not entirely disagreeable, I always respond *yes, yes* in turn.

'Happy New Year,' I replied. 'And what a wonderful new bell you're wearing there.'

'Oh this? My mistress bought it for me at the end of last year. Isn't it darling?' and she gave her bell a little tinkle as she spoke.

'Indeed. It truly is a pretty sound. In all my life I don't think I've ever laid eyes on such a pretty thing.'

'Oh come now! Everyone's got them these days.' And again she gave a little tinkle. 'It's such a sweet sound. I'm *so* happy with it.' She continued to let it jingle and jangle.

'Your mistress really must adore you,' I said, slightly revealing my covert envy.

But Miss Calico, being a simple and pure soul, replied, 'She really does. She treats me as if I were her own child.' She laughed innocently.

Just because we are cats, it doesn't mean we cannot laugh. The absurd idea humans have – that they are the only animal who laughs – is an entirely fallacious one. When we laugh, our nostrils take on a triangular shape and we give off subtle vibrations from the depths of our throats. That's probably why humans don't notice.

'What's the story with the master of your household?' I asked.

'Master of my household? That's a funny thing to say. She's my *mistress* and she's just a humble teacher of the koto. She specializes in teaching the two-string koto, to be precise.'

'I know all that. That much I have observed. But what I meant is, what's her lineage? She must have been of noble birth originally, before the restoration of the Emperor Meiji.'

'Oh, yes.'

'*In the shade of the white pine grove,*
I pine for you . . .~♪'

Through a gap in the shoji sliding paper doors came the sound of the koto, accompanied by her voice.

'Isn't she just amazingly talented?' boasted Miss Calico with obvious pride.

'It's lovely, but I'm really no expert. What's the song she's singing called?'

'Hmm . . . that song? Oh, that's called . . . a song . . . called . . . something or other . . . that she likes to play . . . Um, she's sixty-two, did you know that? Doesn't she look absolutely *marvellous* for her age?'

As far as I was concerned, anyone still living at the age of sixty-two was doing well.

'Yes,' I replied.

It was a bit of an idiotic response, but I didn't really have anything else to say.

'But, as we were saying,' said Miss Calico. 'She's from a very noble lineage. She tells me about it from time to time.'

'Oh really? Who is she related to?'

'She's the shogun's wife's secretary's sister's mother-in-law's nephew's daughter, apparently.'

'Uh, say again?'

'Right . . . The shogun's wife's secretary's sister's mother-in-law's —'

'Wait, wait, I think I have it. Just a second. The shogun's wife's sister's secretary's —'

'No! The shogun's wife's secretary's sister's —'

'Got it. The . . . shogun's . . . wife's, right?'

'Right.'

'Secretary's . . .?'

'Correct.'

'Mother's . . .?'

'Mother-*in-law's*.'

'Yes, yes. I messed up there. Mother-in-law's . . .'

'Nephew's daughter.'

'Mother-in-law's nephew's daughter. Is that right?'

'Perfect. You got it.'

'Hmm . . . I'm still not entirely clear. I'm a little confused. What does that make the shogun's wife to her, then?'

'Ugh! You really don't understand at all, do you? Silly! Like I said before, she's the shogun's wife's secretary's sister's mother-in-law's nephew's daughter! Haven't I been telling you that this whole time?'

'I understand that much, but —'

'Well, that's really all there is to it.'

'Fantastic,' I said, finally admitting defeat. Some-times honesty is *not* the best policy.

From behind the sliding doors the sound of the koto abruptly stopped and was replaced by the koto teacher's calling voice.

'Kitty-chan! Oh, Kitty-chan! Time for din-dins!'

Miss Calico looked over the moon.

'Oh! That's my mistress calling me, I have to go home now. Is that all right?' It wasn't as if I could say no. 'Do come visit again soon, won't you?'

She tinkled her bell as she made her way through the garden towards the house, but then suddenly turned and came back to me.

'By the way, Professor, you seem a little out of sorts today. Are you all right? Did something happen?' she asked, with an expression of concern.

I couldn't exactly tell her I'd eaten some cursed mochi and danced with the devil.

'Nothing especially . . . I suppose I did some heavy philosophical thinking earlier, which made my head hurt a tiny bit, but I thought if I came and had a chat with you I'd feel right as rain in no time. That's why I came to visit.'

'Yes. Well, take good care of yourself. Bye for now,' she said with a tinge of regret at having to leave. And with that, I felt fully recovered from the mochi episode of earlier.

I was feeling sprightly again. So much so, that

on my way home I thought I'd cut through the tea garden. As I was trampling on some frost needles I stuck my head through the ancient dilapidated fence and once again saw the rickshaw man's cat, Mr Kuro, on top of the withered chrysanthemums, arching his back like a mountain in a long-drawn-out yawn. I'm no longer scared of Mr Kuro, but getting into a conversation with him is really quite tiresome, so I made as if I hadn't seen him and carried on my way. He's the type who cannot even stand the thought that someone might be looking down on him, so he didn't stay silent for long.

'Oi! Yeah, you, Mr No-named Nobody! You really fink yer somefing special these days, don'tcha? Swannin' around with that smug mug. Well, it don't matter 'ow much teacher's nosh yer chow down on, that don't change nuffin'. You ain't so great, matey!'

It appeared Mr Kuro had absolutely no idea just how famous I've become of late. Even if I wanted to explain this to him, he's not the kind of fellow who would understand these sorts of things, so I decided to offer him a formal greeting for the time being, so that I might get away from him sooner.

'Happy New Year, Mr Kuro. You're looking well, as ever,' I said, raising my tail and leaning it to the left in salutation. Mr Kuro, however, did not return the gesture.

'Whasso 'appy about it? I bet yer the kind of

idiot 'oos still saying 'appy New Year in April. Get stuffed! Yer'd better watch yersself, yer back-end-of-a-bellows-faced nitwit.'

This *back-end-of-a-bellows-faced nitwit* sounded like an insult to me, but I couldn't quite understand exactly what it meant.

'What would the back end of a bellows look like on a nitwit? I can't quite picture it.'

'You really are a new kind of stupid, ain'tcha? Yer being called names, but yer wants to know what the names *mean* — well, it *means* yer a New Year's numbskull.'

A *New Year's numbskull* (while I did appreciate the alliterative nature) was perhaps even more unclear an image than all that back-end-of-a-bellows stuff. Despite wanting further clarification, it was clear I wasn't going to get any kind of useful response, and so I stood stock-still, facing him, and said nothing. I wasn't really sure what to do next. But then suddenly Mr Kuro's mistress screamed loudly.

''Ere! Where's that salmon I put on the counter?! Bastard! I bet that beast of a cat has nicked it again. 'Ee's an 'orrible cat, I tells yer! When 'ee gets back I'll show 'im a thing or two,' she shouted.

And thus, that tranquil New Year's calm was unceremoniously shattered; a reign of natural peace, when all was well with the world, just like that, was instantly debased. Mr Kuro wore a lazy, impudent expression on his face that said, clear as day: *if you're going to shout, go ahead and scream your head off, lady*, and he jutted out his square jaw at me as if to enquire whether I was hearing all this. I hadn't noticed during my current interaction with Mr Kuro, but I now realized that all this time he had been rolling the bones of a cheap cut of salmon around in the dirt with his front paw.

'Impressive, as always!' I said in admiration, forgetting the awkward exchange we'd been having until now. This, however, was not enough to cheer up Mr Kuro.

'What yer on about *impressive*, yer bastard? What's so *impressive* about a cut or two of salmon? Yer always looking down on people, ain'tcha? Let me remind yer 'oo I am – I'm the famous Mr Kuro the rickshaw man's cat!' And with that he lifted his left paw and brushed his right arm menacingly, all the way up to his shoulder, as though rolling up his sleeve for a scrap.

'I'm well aware of who you are, Mr Kuro.'

'If yer knows already, what's all this rot about swipin' some measly salmon being *impressive*?' And he began to hiss hotly at me.

If we were humans, he probably would've grabbed me by my lapels and started shoving me about. I was feeling rather at a loss as to what to do, but then the shrill voice of Mr Kuro's mistress rang out again.

'Nishikawa-san! 'Ey! Nishikawa-san! Are yer deaf,

man? I'm talking to yer. I've got a job for you. Fetch me a cut of beef. All right? You got it? A pound of beef, and none of the tough stuff, mind!' The sound of her beef order echoed around the peaceful street.

'Hmph. She only orders beef once a year, so that's why she's shouting so bloody loud about it. The old trout is boasting to the 'ole neighbourhood about one tiddly tiny pound of beef,' said Mr Kuro scornfully, while stretching all four limbs.

I wasn't sure what to say, so I just kept quiet.

'One paltry pound . . . Oh well, it'll 'ave to do. I'll be 'aving that when 'ee gets back wiv it,' he said, as though the order of beef had been made for himself alone.

'Sounds like you're in for a feast! Splendid, splendid,' I said, trying to get him to leave faster.

'What the 'ell do you know? Shut yer cakehole! Know-it-all!' he said, while suddenly kicking up some fallen frost needles with his hind legs, showering my head in ice.

Shocked, I shook the slush from my body, and while I was doing so, Mr Kuro ducked under a hedge and disappeared. I presumed he was off to swipe Nishikawa-san's beef.

When I returned to the household, I was greeted with the slightly uncharacteristic cheer of the New Year season. I even heard the sound of my master laughing.

To my surprise, the doors were all wide open, and I made my way through them via the wooden veranda, expecting to sit at my master's side, only to see we had an unfamiliar visitor. His hair was parted neatly, and he wore a crested cotton haori overcoat along with a pair of hakama wide-pleated trousers, produced in the town of Kokura in Kyushu. The fellow had all the outward appearances of an extremely earnest student. On the master's small brazier I could see a business card lined up next to his lacquered cigarette holder, and on it was written:

I do humbly introduce 越智東風
Yours, Kangetsu Mizushima

From this I could not only infer the visitor's name in kanji, which I read as Ochi Tofu,[1] but also the fact that he was a friend of Kangetsu-kun's. I'd stumbled into the conversation between guest and host mid-flow, so wasn't quite sure what had come before this, but I could tell that the subject of it now pertained to the art critic Meitei-kun, who you'll remember I've made mention of several times before.

'. . . and then he says, "*I've got a wonderful caper planned, Ochi-kun, so do come along with me, won't you?*" ' said the visitor, calmly.

---

1 Japanese names written in kanji can be read in multiple different ways. The cat has made an educated guess, but it is not necessarily the correct reading.

'And what did this *caper* involve, I wonder? Going to a Western restaurant for lunch?' asked the master, pushing a cup of tea towards the guest.

'Yes, but at that time, I had literally no idea what he had in store. At any rate, I was pretty sure that whatever scheme the chap cooked up was going to be a hoot . . .'

'So you went along to the restaurant together, I see.'

'. . . but what he had planned surprised even me.'

The master tapped me on the head sharply at this point, as if to say, *Did you hear that?* The tap hurt a bit. 'Once again, he's come up with some farcical trick, I'll bet. That man really has issues,' said the master, clearly recalling the Andrea del Sarto incident.

'*Heh heh*. Quite. And then he says, "*Let's eat something really weird.*"'

'What did you have?'

'Well, first he studies the menu and reels off a load of stories, explaining to me every little thing he knows about Western food.'

'Before ordering?'

'Yep.'

'And then?'

'Then he cocks his head to one side and calls out to the waiter, and asks him if they don't have anything a little more exciting than what's on the menu, to which the waiter (not wanting to be outdone) replies by suggesting the specials – roast duck, veal chops and so forth. But before he can finish, Meitei-sensei interrupts and says, "*Look, man, we didn't come all this way for that clichéd stuff.*" The waiter, either not understanding the word *clichéd* or failing to see how any of that Western food could be considered so, pulls an odd face and stands there in silence.'

'Rightly so.'

'Then Meitei-sensei turns to me and launches into a long diatribe. "*If one goes to France or England, the menus there read like divine works of literature – pure poetry – written in the elaborate and original hand of the author!*" he says. "*Whereas in Japan, menus read like a mass-produced, shoddy first print run of a penny dreadful, and that, dear fellow, is why I don't frequent Western restaurants in Japan –*" By the way, Sensei, has that chap ever been abroad?'

'Meitei-san? Abroad? Pah! Not on your life. He's got the money, he's got the time, and he talks about wanting to go a lot, but he's still yet to take the plunge. Perhaps, for the purposes of this jape, he thought to *present* his *future* plans as *past* experiences,' said the master, laughing out loud and obviously thinking he'd said something witty. The guest did not appear impressed.

'Right . . . well, you see . . . I was under the impression he'd been abroad at some point or other, and so against my better judgement I, um, I listened to him in all earnestness. Because, well, he even went so far as describing (in great detail, mind) tales of trying slug soup and frog stew on his travels.'

'He'd probably heard all that from someone else, we all know he's famous for telling porky pies.'

'Yes, yes. You're probably right,' the guest said, gazing at a vase of daffodils. He appeared a little dejected.

'So that was the end of the *caper*?' prompted the master.

'Oh . . . not at all. That was just the appetizer, so to speak. The main course is yet to come.'

'Hmm,' the master murmured in curiosity.

'So, then he finishes off his spiel about Western restaurants, saying that if we can't have slugs or frogs today, how about having some delicious *beet mauls* instead, which he carefully pronounces in what I think is English, and I (once again against my better judgement) casually said that why, yes, that would be lovely.'

'*Beet mauls*? Never heard of them. Mauled beetroot? Sounds a little fishy to me . . .'

'Oh, entirely. As fishy as a fish market, but you must understand, Meitei-sensei is saying all this with a dead straight face, so I think absolutely nothing of it.' The visitor made excuses, as though apologizing to the master for his carelessness.

'And then what happened?' asked the master with

indifference. He appeared to entertain no sympathy towards the guest's excuses.

'Then he calls out to the waiter, and tells him to bring out two orders of their finest beet mauls, to which the waiter responds, asking if he doesn't perhaps mean *meatballs*. With a deadly serious face, Meitei-sensei replies in turn that no, he doesn't mean meatballs, thank you very much, he *means* beet mauls.'

'Hmm. And do these beet mauls even exist?'

'Well, yes, I thought they sounded a little strange, too, but Meitei-sensei was so calmly adamant about it all, and he's apparently very knowledgeable about all things Western. Bear in mind, at that time, I was under the impression he'd even spent time abroad, and so I hummed in agreement with him, even going so far as trying to teach the waiter a thing or two, saying, *"Not meatballs, chappy, we want beet mauls, that's right, beet mauls."'*

'And how did the waiter respond?'

'The waiter . . .? Ah, when I think about the whole thing now, it really is quite hilarious . . . he stands there for a minute, giving it some careful thought and deliberation, then says in a very contrite manner, *"I'm terribly sorry, my dear sirs, we're unfortunately out of beet mauls for today, but if you'd like meatballs, we can prepare those for you instantly."* To which Meitei-sensei pulls a desperately forlorn face, and says, *"Oh no . . . such a shame. We've come all this way for nothing. Look, man, are you sure there's nothing to be done about those beet mauls? There's a good fellow,"* and with that he gives the waiter a twenty-sen silver coin, at which point the waiter goes to the kitchen to have a word with the chef.'

'Seems like he really had a hankering for beet mauls.'

'After some time, the waiter returns and tells us that he really is sorry, but if that's what we want, it will unfortunately take quite some time to prepare, to which Meitei-sensei calmly says, "*Oh, that's quite all right. It's New Year's after all, so we don't have anything to do especially. We'll be absolutely fine waiting.*" With that, he takes out a cigarette from the jacket pocket of his Western suit and begins puffing away contentedly, and I, unsure what else to do, pull out my copy of the *Japan News* from the fold in my kimono and start to read it. Once again, the waiter retreats to the kitchen for a pep talk with the chef.'

'Wow. You really put them through the wringer!' said the master, sitting forward in his seat, as though he were hearing some kind of gripping war report newly delivered from the front line.

'The waiter reappears, and says that he really is terribly sorry, but as of late the ingredients for beet mauls are so scarce and hard to come by that, for the time being, one cannot even find them in a big store such as Kameya, and even going all the way to the imported goods shops of Yokohama, one is likely to come back empty-handed. Meitei-sensei says, "*Oh no! What a shame! We came all this way!*" And he keeps turning and looking my way, expecting me to say something, and I can't very well just sit there in silence, so I say, "*Yes, it really is a shame. I'm so disappointed,*" purely to match his mood.'

'Which is only natural,' agrees the master.

I personally can't see what is *natural* about any of this shaggy-dog nonsense.

'Meanwhile, the waiter looks sympathetic, and says that when they do get the ingredients in stock we really must come again to sample the delicious beet mauls. At that, Meitei-sensei asks what ingredients they use for beet mauls at that particular restaurant, to which the poor waiter can only laugh nervously, *heh, heh, heh* . . . Meitei-sensei persists, and asks, "*I expect you use only haiku poets of the Japan-style?*" to which the waiter says, "*Yes, sir, you're quite right. And recently you can't even get hold of those in Yokohama, which is such a shame.*" '

'Ah ha ha ha! And that's the twist? That is hilarious!' said the master in an uncharacteristically loud voice, roaring with laughter. His knees were shaking so violently I thought I might fall off. Despite this, he carried on laughing in a carefree manner. I'm certain he'd only cheered up so suddenly upon seeing he wasn't the only dope to fall foul of a prank like the Andrea del Sarto incident.

'After that we leave the restaurant, and Meitei-sensei turns to me and says, "*So, how was that? I thought you put in a great performance. We put those beet mauls to good work, didn't we, eh?*" His face was beaming, like the cat who got the cream. We parted ways, and although I felt a deep sense of admiration at his little caper, it was now well past lunchtime, and I had grown quite weak with hunger.'

'That must've been awful,' said the master, finally showing some compassion. I could empathize, too, as it really *is* awful to miss a meal. The conversation paused for a short time, and the only noise that could be heard by host and guest was the sound of my soft purring.

Tofu-kun glugged his tepid tea down in one go.

'The truth is, Sensei, the real reason I came today was to ask a favour,' he said, changing the topic.

'Go on . . .' said the master expectantly.

'As you well know, I'm a big fan of the arts and literature –'

'And a wonderful thing that is, too,' the master piled it on a little thickly.

'Yes, well, I got together with some like-minded fellows and we've established a reading group, we plan to meet up once a month and practise together, we had our first ever meeting at the end of last year.'

'Just a sec, when you say *reading group*, am I right in thinking it's the sort of thing where you practise the recitation and rhythms of performing Japanese and Chinese verse – is that it? How do you run it?'

'Well, we're starting off with the classics, and eventually after a bit we plan to even perform original works written by members of the group.'

'When you say the classics, do you mean things like *Ballad of the Lute* by Bai Juyi?'

'No.'

'How about Yosa Buson's *Song of the Spring Wind on the Horse Bank*?'

'No.'

'So what kinds of things are we talking about, then?'

'Last time we did a double love suicide scene from Chikamatsu.'

'Chikamatsu, as in the playwright?'

Now, ladies and gentlemen, there are no two Chikamatsus in existence. When people say *Chikamatsu*, it's a foregone conclusion they're talking about the dramatist. I was thinking to myself how stupid the master sounded by asking this question, when he, blissfully ignorant of what I was thinking, lovingly stroked my head. Yet, in a world in which there are many who mistake a cross-eyed person's gaze for admiration, it's no surprise the master would make a blunder like this, so I let him carry on stroking me.

'Yes,' replied Tofu-kun, examining my master's expression carefully.

'So, does just one person read all the lines, or do you divide up characters and take parts that way?'

'Oh, we divvy up roles and take a part each. We make it a priority to empathize with the characters within the story and do our best to inject emotion into the performances. To that end, we add some basic gestures and simple movements. We try to make the lines as authentic to the era as possible, whether it's a young lady or a shop boy, we aim to make it seem as though the actual person has appeared before our very eyes.'

'So, like a stage play?'

'Yes, I suppose so, except of course there are no costumes or stage decorations.'

'Bit rude of me to ask, but was it any good?'

'Well, for a first effort, I think it went pretty decently.'

'And what was the scene you mentioned just now . . . something about a double love suicide?'

'Yup, that's the one. About a ferryman taking a passenger to the red-light district in Yoshiwara.'

'Wow, that's quite the production . . .' said the master, inclining his head slightly to one side. He exhaled a cloud of cigarette smoke from his nose, which wreathed around my ear and skimmed its way across my face.

'Really? I didn't think it was such a big deal. Because in terms of cast there's just the ferryman, a courtesan, a hostess, a mama-san and a pimp,' said Tofu-kun nonchalantly.

The master, upon hearing the word 'courtesan', pulled a bitter face, apparently not knowing the exact meanings of words such as hostess, mama-san and pimp. He first asked a question.

'And is a hostess someone who works in a brothel, I wonder?'

'I haven't yet researched the matter, but I believe a hostess is a serving girl in a teahouse, while I think a mama-san is someone who looks after a house of . . . ah . . . ladies.'

Even though Tofu-kun had made claim to manifesting the characters through reciting their words, almost as if they'd appeared before the audience's very eyes, he still seemed a little unsure as to the roles of a mama-san and a hostess.

'I see, so a hostess is under the employ of a teahouse, while a mama-san takes charge of a brothel. But then, I wonder, is a pimp a person or a place? And if it's a person, are they male or female?'

'I'm told a pimp is a male adult — at least, I think so . . .'

'And what does he take charge of, I wonder?'

'I've not looked into the matter that far. We'll have to do a bit more research before long . . .'

On hearing this, I wondered what kind of absurd performance they must've put on that day; I raised my head to take a look at the master's face. Contrary to my expectations, he wore a look of complete sincerity.

'So, other than you, who else was at the reading group?'

'Oh, quite the rag-tag bunch. The courtesan was played by a lawyer, K-kun, but I must say, the effect of his moustache coupled with the effeminate dialogue he read, well, it was all quite odd. And then there was the part where the courtesan has a fit . . .'

'And was it really quite necessary to have an actual fit, even at a reading group?' asked the master in concern.

'Oh absolutely! Expression is everything, after all,' said Tofu-kun, adopting the seasoned air of a true artist, right to the bitter end.

'And was the fit, be*fit*ting?' asked the master in an ironic tone.

'Well, the first time, I must admit, it came in fits and starts,' said Tofu-kun, returning the ironical tone.

'And what part did you play?' asked the master.

'Me? Oh, the ferryman.'

'Hmm . . . So, you were the ferryman,' mused the master, in a way that clearly suggested *if even you could play the ferryman, I could certainly play the pimp.*

A short pause. 'And were you any good?' he asked, bluntly.

Tofu-kun appeared not to have taken any offence. He calmly replied in the same tone as before.

'One might say that, despite my best efforts, the ferryman began like a dragon's roar, and ended like a snake's tail, so to speak. An anti-climax, to say the least. What happened was, next door to the assembly hall we were using, well, it turns out there were four or five schoolgirls staying there at a boarding house. I'm not even sure how they'd found out, but either they'd heard there was a reading group going on that day, or they'd heard our performance and snuck to a spot under the window to eavesdrop on us. Anyhow, I was throwing myself wholeheartedly into the role of the ferryman, and got a little bit carried away with myself, by which I mean that perhaps I overdid it a touch with the gestures. At which point the girls, who had been holding back thus far, let out a fit of giggles all at once. Of course, this took me by complete surprise and caught me off guard, and then with my feathers all ruffled I couldn't exactly find it within me to carry on. So, at that, we called it a day.'

If this first reading group session could be deemed a *success*, I couldn't help but let out a laugh at the thought of what a *failure* might look like. Without thinking about it, I let out a low rumbling of the throat, which the master mistook for a purr. At which he stroked my head even more gently. While I'm grateful that the more I laugh at humans, the more they are inclined to think I'm adorable, all the same, it felt a little unsettling.

'How awful,' said the master, seemingly keen to bring a morbid tone to the Happy New Year as soon as he could.

'From our second meeting, we're aiming to really push the boat out, so to speak, and put everything we've got into it. Actually, that's why I've come to see you today, Sensei. The truth is, we could really do with your assistance, and wonder if you might help us by joining the group . . .'

'I really can't do fits, or anything like that,' said the lazy master, already trying to wriggle his way out of having to do anything.

'No, no, there's no need for fits, we just need you to sign your name in support,' said Tofu-kun, meanwhile taking out an important-looking notebook from a purple furoshiki wrapping. 'We just need your signature, and then a stamp from your official inkan seal.' And with that, he placed the open notebook in front of the master's knees.

Upon inspecting the list, I made out a plethora of names with PhDs and BAs attached, comprising many of the most renowned literary scholars of the age.

'I'm not saying I won't support the cause, but what responsibilities does it entail exactly?' asked Dr Oyster PhD anxiously, with his backside planted firmly on his cushion.

'There are no responsibilities or obligations to

speak of, it would just be enough to sign your name here in support.'

'If that's the case, then I'm happy to sign.' As soon as he found out he didn't have to do anything, he was as happy as a pig in filth. His expression said clearly that he'd sign his name to any cause, even a bloodthirsty rebellion, just so long as he didn't have to lift a finger as a result. Furthermore, seeing the chance to add his name to a list of famous scholars, it was only natural that the master (who had never in his life till now been given such an honour) would rush to sign with such vim and vigour.

'Sorry, just a second,' said the master, going into the study to fetch his official inkan seal.

As he stood, I fell with a splat on to the tatami matting. Tofu-kun took a large piece of Portuguese castella sponge cake from the cake dish and crammed it all in his mouth at once. He munched away on it for quite some time, and began to look a tiny bit distressed. For me, it brought back painful memories of that morning's Mochi Incident. The master emerged from the study with his inkan seal at precisely the same moment that the castella sponge cake dropped into Tofu-kun's stomach. The master apparently didn't notice the huge slice of castella missing from the cake dish. Had he noticed, we all know I would have been the prime suspect.

After Tofu-kun left, the master went into the

study and saw that at some point a letter had arrived on his desk from Meitei-sensei.

Please allow me to take this opportunity to wish you the very happiest of New Year's celebrations during this seasonal period.

This seemed, thought the master to himself, an uncharacteristically serious opening to a letter. When it came to Meitei-sensei and letters, serious ones just didn't exist. The other day the master had received one which, apropos of nothing, simply said:

As of late, I have not a single female admirer. A direct result of which is that I receive no love letters at all, and so I spend my time quite un-eventfully. Please allow me to be so bold as to humbly ask for your peace of mind regarding the matter, because I'm sure you've been worried.

When compared with that sort of humorous nonsense, this particular New Year's letter seemed all the more exceptionally ordinary and mundane.

Though I've very much wanted to call on you, in direct contrast to your pessimistic approach to life I've made a conscious effort and plan of action to be as positive and proactive as possible, namely so that I might welcome in this marvellously unpre-cedented New Year, and day after day my head is sent reeling at how terribly busy I am. Therefore, I do humbly request your understanding.

'Ah, so that's it. Just what I'd expect from that fellow – no doubt he's busy making the rounds at New Year,' the master said to himself, understanding Meitei-sensei's position entirely.

Yesterday, having snatched a moment of respite for myself, I thought to treat young Tofu-kun to some delicious beet mauls. Alas, due to a scarcity of ingredients, to no avail. It was really quite a shame.

'There it is,' said the master quietly to himself, a grin spreading across his face. 'Back to his old self.'

Tomorrow, I'm meeting with a certain Baron for cards, the day after is the Society of Aesthetics' New Year's banquet, after that it's Professor Toribe's welcome party, and then again the next day it's . . .

'Gosh, he does go on a bit,' said the master, obviously skimming over this part.

And so it is with all the groups I'm part of – the Noh singing, tanka poetry, free-form verse and so on – it'll be an endless succession of parties for these societies, and due to my ceaselessly having to put in an appearance at them all, I've been forced to take up my pen and send you this letter in place of a formal visit. I beg you forgive me for this, and hope you understand, please don't think too harshly of me.

'Hold on a second, who on earth ever said you had to come here in the first place?' said the master out loud, as if talking in response to the letter itself.

When next you have occasion to visit, it would be wonderful to dine together as it's been quite some time since we had the pleasure. Despite my stark winter pantry being quite lacking of late, it would be an honour to offer you at the very least some delicious beet mauls . . .

'Again, he's spouting about the beet mauls,' said the master, sounding a little offended. 'I can't believe he thinks I'd fall for that.'

However, due to an unfortunate recent shortage of the ingredients for beet mauls, it's hard to say whether they will be possible or not, depending on circumstances, in which case, I might offer you some peacock tongue for you to sample instead . . .

'Peacock tongue? Another ace up his sleeve,' said the master, eager to read the rest.

As I'm sure you're well aware, one bird only

produces the tiniest amount of tongue meat – no more than half the size of a little finger – which is nowhere near enough to satisfy the stomach of a glutton such as yourself . . .

'Absolute piffle!' let out the master, before continuing.

I estimate I'll need to capture about twenty to thirty birds to cater for you. While they can be found in zoos, and one does catch sight of them here and there at places like Asakusa Amusement Park, the trouble with peacocks is that they're not to be found at all in any ordinary bird dealer's shops, which makes this quite the tricky situation . . .

'A tricky situation of your own concoction, which you've cooked up entirely unnecessarily,' said the master, without showing the least bit of gratitude.

As a dish, peacock tongue dates all the way back to the days of Ancient Rome, at which time during the height of the Roman Empire it really was all the rage. If you would be so kind as to indulge me, please know that I have long had a secret hankering to sample this extravagant and refined luxury . . .

'Indulge him? The only secret hankering he's got is for overindulging in foolishness,' said the master with cool indifference.

As time went on, up until the sixteenth or seventeenth century, peacock tongue was standard fair at banquets throughout the whole of Europe. If memory serves correctly, the Earl of Leicester made use of the pavonine dish when he received Queen Elizabeth at Kenilworth. There's even a famous Rembrandt painting of a banquet in which a peacock is clearly depicted laid out on its back, tail and all, spatchcocked on the tabletop . . .

'If he's got time enough to pen this culinary history of peacock tongue, he really can't be that busy at all,' burst out the master in irritation.

Anyhow, if I carry on feasting at the rate I have of late, it's a sure thing that sometime soon, in the none-too-distant future, little old me will certainly become a dyspeptic, such as yourself . . .

'Really, the "such as yourself" is a little bit uncalled for. There's no need to make me the yardstick for dyspepsia, thank you very much,' muttered the master.

According to historians, the Romans are said to have held as many as two or three banquets in a single day. Now, no matter how strong a person's stomach, if they are to sit at table two or three times a day and stuff themselves with rich food, it's sure to give rise to digestive problems, consequently it was only natural for someone such as yourself . . .

'Again with the "such as yourself". Pure insolence.'

However, in order for them to simultaneously enjoy this level of extravagance while also maintaining their health, they studied the matter to exhaustion. And, in order that they might eat large quantities of rich food, while also preserving a healthy digestive tract, they discovered a secret method . . .

'Did they now?' said the master, suddenly becoming enthusiastic.

After every meal, they would go straight to the baths, without fail. After bathing, they would, by using a certain method, vomit everything they'd consumed before they'd taken their bath, thereby cleansing the stomach. Once they had purged their stomachs, they could once again return to the table, indulge in rich foods until satiated, and then, having enjoyed the food, once again return to the baths to disgorge themselves. In this manner, they could eat as much of their favourite foods as they wanted, without damaging their digestive tract – literally having their cake and eating it, if you will . . .

'Well I never, that certainly is having your cake and eating it, make no mistake.' The master wore an envious expression on his face.

These days, in the twentieth century, with ever-progressive discourse and, needless to say, an ever-increasing number of banquets (as a nation at war during this second year of the conflict against Russia), I secretly believe that we, the citizens of this victorious nation, must by all means necessary look further into this ancient Roman bathing and vomiting method. For if we do not, I fear the people of this nation might all, in the very near future, inevitably become weak-stomached people, such as yourself . . .

'And there it is again, "such as yourself". What a provocative man,' said the master.

Thus it falls to those of us familiar with the West to research its ancient cultures, to rediscover this lost art of regurgitation, thus putting into play a practical service – an act of charity – that will directly benefit this Meiji society and prevent what is essentially a digestive disaster, but which also might be a means of repaying the debt people like you and I owe to society for what could be considered our past self-indulgent idle pursuits of pleasure . . .

'Well, this is all just bizarre,' said the master, craning his neck.

Consequently, of late I've been meticulously making my way through the works of writers such as Edward Gibbon, Theodor Mommsen, Sir William Smith and others, so that I might discover more about the matter, yet sadly to no avail. But as you well know, I am not the kind of person to give up so easily; once I've put my mind to something, I will pursue the matter to the bitter end. I'm entirely convinced that before very long I shall revive this lost secret art of vomiting. You can rest assured that I will report back to you immediately with any of my findings. Accordingly, I think it might make more sense to postpone the aforementioned beet mauls and peacock tongue until <u>after</u> I've made my breakthrough, as this, it goes without saying, will greatly benefit you, who is – after all is said and done – a man with a weak stomach.

Yours,

Meitei

'What the devil?! Ugh. I've been had again. He wrote it all in such a serious manner that I ended up reading the whole thing right through to the end in earnest. He really does have too much time on his hands to be going to such lengths with his New Year's pranks,' said the master while laughing.

After that, some four or five days passed by quite uneventfully. The daffodil in the white porcelain vase withered gradually, and I spent dull days simply watching the progress of the still-green buds of the plum blossom slowly opening, at which point I thought I might call on Miss Calico. However, despite going to the house, I didn't manage to meet with her. At first I thought she was out, but the second time I called on her I discovered she had been unwell and was sleeping. While I was hiding in the shade of the aspidistra, through a gap in the shoji sliding doors I overheard a conversation between the koto teacher and her maid.

'Has Kitty-chan eaten her din-dins?'

'No, she still hasn't eaten since this morning. I settled her down to sleep in the warmth of the kotatsu.'

It didn't sound at all like they were talking about a cat. They treated her as if she were a fellow human.

On the one hand it made me feel slightly envious of her when I compared her life to my own situation, but on the other it made me happy to hear that the cat I loved was being treated so well.

'Oh, that is worrying, isn't it? If she doesn't eat properly, she won't regain her strength.'

'You're quite right, ma'am. I'm just the same – if I don't eat for even a day, the next morning I can barely move my body.'

The maid spoke of the cat as if she were of a higher social standing than herself. Perhaps in this household cats were considered more important than maids.

'And did you take her to the doctor?'

'Yes, ma'am. But he was a funny one. When I carry Kitty-chan into his examination room in my arms, he asks me if I've caught a cold and tries to take my pulse. No, I says, I'm not the patient. And I sets Kitty-chan on my knees for him to take a look at her. He smirks at me and says, "*I have no idea how to treat a cat, but it can't be that serious, just leave it be and I'm sure it'll get better in no time.*" Can you believe it? Isn't that awful? I got angry, I says, "*She is a very important cat, so we won't be needing your help, thank you very much,*" and with that I tuck her into the breast of my kimono and bring her straight home.'

'Truly beastly man!'

Truly beastly man is not the kind of elegant turn of phrase one would ever hear in our household. But I would expect nothing less in terms of refinement from someone who happened to be the shogun's wife's . . . something or other. I was extremely impressed at her nobility.

'She's making that somewhat strange weeping sound. There, do you hear?'

'Yes, ma'am! It must be a cold and it's given her a

ghastly sore throat, I'll bet. Colds are tricksy things . . . howsoever one treats them, they're bound to lead to a cough, too.'

'*Ghastly*'? '*Howsoever*'? It seemed that even the shogun's wife's something or other's maid is also required to lay on this absurdly ridiculous, posh manner of speaking.

'And then there's bronchitis doing the rounds these days . . .'

'Oh, absolutely, ma'am, and there are all these new illnesses on the rise like tuberculosis and the bubonic plague, and if we're not careful they'll find their way into our household.'

'Things are not as they were in the days of the Shogun. Without honourable people to protect us, you must be careful, my dear.'

'You're quite right, ma'am.'

The maid seemed deeply moved.

'Although, it *is* strange that Kitty-chan would catch a cold, because she doesn't often take her perambulations outdoors, does she?'

'Very true, ma'am, although . . . now that you come to mention it, she's made *an undesirable friend* of late.'

The maid's tone changed, as if she were divulging a national secret. She looked far too pleased with herself.

'An undesirable friend?'

'Yes, it's that filthy-looking tomcat who lives in the teacher's house on the main street.'

'When you say teacher, do you mean that ill-mannered brute who makes such a frightful racket each and every morning?'

'Yes! That's the one – the fellow who makes a noise like a strangled goose every time he washes his face.'

A noise like a strangled goose was actually a fitting description. My master has taken to the bizarre habit of tapping his neck with his toothbrush while he gargles in the bathroom, producing quite an unseemly noise. When he's in a bad mood, he gargles with vehemence, and when he's in a good mood his gargle takes on an even louder, croakier timbre. In other words, whether he is in a good mood or a bad one, the force and vigour of his gargling is relentless. According to the mistress, before they moved into this new house he didn't have this nasty habit, but it seems he started one day and hasn't given it a day's rest ever since. And even though it's a really obnoxious habit, why he continues to pursue it with such devotion, I, as a mere cat, could not possibly imagine. That's all well and good, but my ears really pricked up when I heard the words *filthy-looking tomcat*, which I thought extremely harsh and slightly unfair criticism. Nevertheless, I continued eavesdropping.

'Who knows what kind of malediction he's making when he lets out that awful sound. In the good old days of the Shogun, before the Restoration, even a samurai's footmen – heck, even a sandal carrier – knew their place and how to conduct themselves properly. There wasn't a single person in the residential area who'd wash their face in that odd manner.'

'You're quite right, ma'am.'

The maid, excessively impressed, makes excessive use of the word *ma'am*.

'That cat – with an awful master like that – is no doubt a stray. Next time he shows his face, be sure to give him a good thrashing, will you?'

'Oh, I'll thrash him good and proper, make no mistake. I'd wager for sure that it's entirely down to him that our darling Kitty-chan's health has taken a turn for the worse. I'll get my revenge and thrash him into next week.'

An unexpected false accusation! Judging it best not to get too close to these two, I went home again without meeting Miss Calico.

When I got home, I found the master in his study meditating over some written composition with his pen in his hand. If he'd got wind of the conversation I'd overheard just now at the koto teacher's house, he would've flown into a rage, but as they say, *ignorance is bliss*. And right now he had all the air and dignity of a poet, hmm-hmming over his work.

Shortly thereafter, who should stroll into the study

in an aloof manner but the very man who had gone out of his way to write a New Year's card expressly stating that he couldn't visit because he was far too busy. This very same Meitei-sensei sat down casually and made himself at home.

'What are you writing? Some new style of poetry, I shouldn't wonder. If you write anything good, show it to me, won't you?' he said.

'Hmm, I found an interesting piece of prose, so I thought I'd try my hand at translating it,' said the master gloomily, finally opening his mouth.

'Prose? Whose prose?'

'No idea.'

'Anonymous-san, eh? Well, Anonymous-san is responsible for some of our finest works, so he can't exactly be made fun of now, can he? Where did you get this piece?' he asked.

'From the *Second Reader*,' answered the master calmly.

'The second reader? What do you need a second reader for?'

'The famous piece I'm translating, I came across it in a book of extracts called *Second Reader*.'

'Wait, you're not pulling my leg, are you? Are you trying to get your own back, after the event, for all the peacock tongue stuff?'

'I – unlike you – am not a bullshitter,' said the master, twisting his moustache. He was surprisingly calm.

'In the olden days, it is said that someone asked the poet Rai Sanyo, "*Sensei, have you read anything good of late?*" In response to which he produced a promissory note written in the hand of a packhorse man, insisting it was the best thing he'd read in years. So perhaps your eye for beauty is not so contrary to expectations. Anyhow, read a bit for me, will you? And then I shall give you my thoughts,' said Meitei-sensei, as if he were the arbiter of good literary taste.

The master began to read aloud in a voice more befitting a priest reading the deathbed rites to a dying Zen master.

'Giant . . . Gravity.'

'What the devil is giant gravity?'

'*Giant Gravity* is the title.'

'That's an odd title . . . I don't really get it.'

'It refers to a giant whose name is Gravity.'

'A bit of an ambiguous title, but let's put that aside for now. Read on to the main part. It's very entertaining to listen to, as you have such a wonderful voice.'

'Less of your nonsense,' the master warned, and then he continued to read.

Kate looks out of the window. Children are playing with a ball. They throw it high up into the air. Up and up it goes. And then it starts to fall. Up again they throw it. Once again, for a third time. Each time they throw it up, it falls back down.

'Why does it fall? Why doesn't it keep on going up and up?' asks Kate.

'Because there's a giant who lives inside the Earth,' answers her mother. 'He is Giant Gravity. He is strong. He can pull anything. He holds our house fast to the ground. If he didn't, it would fly away. The children would all fly away, too. Look there, at those leaves falling from the tree. That happens because Giant Gravity is calling them. Whenever you drop a book, that's because Giant Gravity told it to come. The ball goes into the sky. Giant Gravity calls it. And when he calls, it falls.'

'Is that it?'

'Mmm-hmm. Isn't it brilliant?'

'Well, well, well . . . I am impressed. You really got me. This is you getting even after all that beet mauls stuff, isn't it? Well done.'

'I'm not getting even. I really thought it was good, and so I translated it. You don't think so?' said the master, peering into those gold-rimmed spectacles.

'I am shocked. No, I'm impressed – you really had me this time. Well played, well played, indeed . . .' Meitei-sensei nodded, all the while speaking to himself.

The master was not cottoning on at all.

'What are you on about *well played*? I merely

thought it was an interesting piece of prose, so I thought I'd try my hand at translating it, that's all.'

'No, no. It really is quite amazing. I didn't see this coming one bit. I'm embarrassed.'

'No need to be embarrassed at all. Since I gave up the watercolours recently, I thought I'd try my hand at prose instead.'

'And this prose cannot be compared to your watercolours, which I must say lacked perspective and balance when it came to light and shade. But this, no, this is something else entirely. I'm very impressed.'

'When you praise me like that, it makes me all the more enthusiastic,' said the master, oblivious to the last.

Shortly thereafter, Kangetsu-kun entered the room.

'Hello, Kangetsu-kun. We have just been hearing a bit of first-class prose that firmly bids farewell to the departed soul of beet mauls,' said Meitei-sensei, hinting obliquely at some obscure matter not shared with the new arrival.

'Hah, is that so?' retorted Kangetsu-kun, in obvious incomprehension.

It was only the master who seemed to derive a sense of pride from the occasion.

'Yesterday, some fellow named Ochi Tofu or something or other came to see me, upon your introduction.'

'Ah, so he came, did he? The kanji for his name is read Ochi *Kochi*, by the way, and he is an upstanding, decent fellow, all right, although he does have his peculiarities . . . I was a little worried he might be bothersome to you, but he really was insistent on making your acquaintance.'

'Oh, he was harmless, not a bother in the slightest . . .'

'He didn't bang on about his name, did he?'

'No . . . It didn't come up at all, actually.'

'Ah, right. Well, he has this awful habit of going into great detail explaining his name whenever he first meets people.'

'What kind of explanation?' asked Meitei-sensei, obviously hoping for some fresh amusement.

'He feels awfully put out if anyone misreads the kanji for his given name *Kochi* as *Tofu*.'

'Good gracious!' said Meitei-sensei, taking a pipe from its fashionable leather and gold case.

'He'll inform them, without fail, "*My name is not Ochi **Tofu**, it's Ochi **Kochi**.*"'

'Bizarre,' said Meitei-sensei, inhaling deeply on a cloud of smoke.

'It all stems from his passion for the written word. If you read his given name as Kochi it sounds like the old poetic expression, written with different characters,' and here Kangetsu-kun wrote the two Chinese characters on a piece of paper: 遠近. 'It's read as *ochikochi* – meaning something like *hither and thither*, or *near and far* – not only that but he's apparently extremely pleased with the way it makes his full name rhyme. That's why, if you really want to rub him up the wrong way, all you have to do is misread his given name as Tofu.'

'My my, an oddball, and no mistake,' said Meitei-sensei, getting so carried away in his amusement that he attempted to snort smoke out of his nostrils from deep within his chest. But the smoke got lost on the way out, and ended up getting caught in his throat. He grasped his pipe tightly and choked back fits of coughing.

'The other day he came to tell me he'd played a ferryman at his reading group, and had been laughed at by a bunch of schoolgirls,' said the master while laughing.

'*Uh huh, yup yup,*' said Meitei-sensei, banging out his pipe on his knee. (I thought this a little dangerous, so moved away from him.) 'Oh, the reading group . . . the other day, when I treated Ochi to some delicious beet mauls, that story came up. I heard they intend to invite well-known men of letters to their next per-formance. He was saying, "*Sensei, we'd be honoured to have you join us.*" Then, when I asked him if they were going to perform another one of Chikamatsu's slice-of-Edo-life dramas, he said no, that they'd decided to do something contemporary and had chosen to perform the novel *The Golden Demon* by Ozaki Koyo. When I asked him what part he was to play, he said the Princess. Princess Tofu must be a sight for sore eyes, I'll bet. I'm definitely planning on attending and have already decided to give a standing ovation.'

'How funny . . .' said Kangetsu-kun, letting out a curious chuckle.

'But that fellow is extremely sincere, he doesn't have a frivolous bone in his body. A good chap, through and through – cut from completely different cloth to someone like Meitei, eh?' said the master, exacting his revenge for Andrea del Sarto, peacock tongue and beet mauls, all together in one fell swoop. Meitei-sensei appeared not to take any notice.

'Yes, I suppose I'm what they commonly refer to as an *Enlightened Chopping Board*, don't you think?'

'Yes, absolutely. I'd say so,' said the master.

Truth be told, he had absolutely no idea what the phrase *Enlightened Chopping Board* meant. However, many years of being a teacher had trained him well in the art of muddying the waters, employing smoke and mirrors and the like – at times like this, his professional life had practical application in social situations.

'What does an *Enlightened Chopping Board* mean?' asked Kangetsu quite frankly.

The master looked in the direction of the tokonoma alcove.

'See that daffodil? I bought that when I was coming home from an evening bath at the end of last year, but it's really holding up well,' he said, forcibly twisting the subject as far away from enlightened chopping boards as he could.

'Speaking of the end of last year, I had a really strange experience in the lead-up to the New Year,' said Meitei, spinning his pipe skilfully in his hand.

'What kind of experience? Let us hear it at once,' said the master, breathing a sigh of relief at having put enlightened chopping boards as far behind him as possible.

And so we listened to Meitei-sensei's strange experience, which happened as follows.

'If memory serves, it must've been the twenty-seventh. I'd received a note from Tofu-kun asking me to stay home that day, as he wanted to call on me to discuss matters pertaining to literature with me, and so from the morning I stayed home waiting, and yet the young master did not appear. I ate lunch, and was reading the humorous stories of Barry Pain in front of the hearth, at which point a letter came from my mother in Shizuoka, which I immediately began to read. She is quite elderly now, but still treats me like a child. She warned me about various things, such as going out late at night during this cold season, and advised that taking a cold bath was fine, but that I must be sure to heat the room I bathed in beforehand, lest I catch a cold, amongst other bits and pieces of advice. It really made me feel appreciative of my parents, and while others may have felt differently, for an idler like myself I was greatly moved at that time. And the more and more I thought about it, the more my aimless life felt like a wasted gift. I felt that I must create some great work of literature, if only for the sake of the family name. I began to feel that I must, while my mother was still alive, make the name of *Meitei* world-famous amongst the literary circles of the Meiji era.

'As I continued to read the letter, my mother went on to point out how lucky a person I am. She wrote that while many young men of the country toil and give their lives in the name of the nation during the war against Russia, I spend each and every day as if it were a holiday, carefree and happy-go-lucky – I should add that I *personally* don't feel I'm as shiftless and idle as my mother makes out – and she then went on to list all of my childhood peers from elementary school who had either died in the war or been mortally wounded. While reading that list of names I began to feel the world a decidedly dull, insipid place – and humans to be a wretched lot. And then, to top it all off, at the end of the letter she says, *and I fear this New Year's mochi rice cake may well be my last* . . . Well, it really was a most forlorn and hopeless letter, and I began to feel extremely depressed, all the while hoping that Tofu-kun might turn up soon and distract me from it all, but alas, the young master did not appear.

'Before long, it was supper time, and I thought I might write a reply to my mother, but I only managed a dozen or so lines. My mother's letter was well over six feet in length, but I could never manage such a performance in response. I got to about ten lines or so before finding a good excuse to end the letter. I'd spent the whole day without any exercise, and was feeling restless to my core. I decided that if young Tofu did come, he could damn well wait a bit, and that I would in the meantime make a trip to the post office to send the letter I'd written, and thus stretch my legs a little at the same time. For some strange reason, though, I found my legs taking me on a different route to normal – instead of my usual trip to Fujimi-cho I found myself heading in the direction of Dotesanban-cho, yet for what reason even I myself could not say. That evening was a little cloudy, and a bitter dry wind blew over the moat, making for an unusually chilly air. A steam train coming from the direction of Kagurazaka rushed by along the embankment, sounding its whistle in a shrill *pyuuuu*. Everything felt lonesome and desolate. The twilight of the year, death in battle, senility, the terrifyingly fleeting nature of life, thoughts like these flooded my head and sloshed around incessantly. I began to recall how many people, at such times as these when overwhelmed by negative thoughts, often become seduced by the idea of hanging themselves to end it all. And then, as I craned my own neck and looked up at the embankment, it was then, and only then, that I realized I found myself right beneath *that* pine tree –'

'*That* pine tree? What are you on about?' asked the master, butting in.

'Hang-Neck Pine,' said Meitei, miming strangling himself by his lapels.

'Wait, Hang-Neck Pine is in Konodai, isn't it?' said Kangetsu, throwing his hat into the ring, too.

'The one in Konodai is Hang-*Bell* Pine, Hang-*Neck* Pine is in Dotesanban-cho. They say the reason why it has this name is because it has long been told that whoever finds themself standing at the base of that particular pine tree is overcome with the uncontrollable urge to hang themself from its boughs. There are any number of pines that line the embankment of Dotesanban-cho, but whenever someone is found hanged, without fail, it's always from this very same tree. There are as many as two or three hangings each year. And for some reason it happens with no other pine. The more I looked at it, the more I imagined its branches reaching out happily to the passers-by, invitingly. Ah! It was a most agreeably shaped tree. I felt it would be a terrible shame to leave it alone like that. I wanted to see what it would look like with a human hanging from its branches, and I wondered if someone might come along soon to fulfil my wish, but when I looked about, sadly no one was coming. There was nothing for it, I'd have to offer up myself . . .

'But, no, no, I conjectured, if I did that, I'd lose my life. However, I remembered then a story of the Ancient Greeks, how they would perform a fake hanging at a banquet as entertainment. A person would get up on a stool and put their neck in a noose, meanwhile another person would sneak up behind and kick the stool out from under them suddenly. And as soon as the stool was kicked, by design, the man who'd put his neck in the noose would slip the knot and fall down to the floor unharmed. If I could do something like that, there'd be nothing to fear, and so I put my hand on the branch to see how it felt – it flexed wonderfully. The flex on the branch was really something else – aesthetic beauty at its finest. Oh, to suspend one's neck from this branch! Well, I began to imagine that pleasant floating sensation buoyed aloft by the branch, the thought of it alone brought me endless delight. I resolved to try it, but then I remembered Tofu-kun – what a shame it would be if he'd come all the way to my house and was waiting there for me now. So, I decided to first meet with Tofu as promised, have that chat, and then I could come back and get on with hanging myself. And so I went home.'

'And you all lived happily ever after?' asked the master.

'Intriguing!' said Kangetsu while grinning.

'When I returned to the house, there was no sign of Tofu. However, there was a postcard from him saying that unfortunately something had come up and he wasn't able to come over for a conversation after all, but that he hoped we might meet soon. At last, I felt relief, I was happy that I could go hang myself without reservation or regret. I immediately slipped into my wooden geta clogs and hurried back to the pine at a fast pace, and there it was I saw . . .' he paused, all the while observing the faces of the master and Kangetsu.

'Yes, you saw . . .? What did you see?' said the master, becoming a little impatient.

'We've finally come to the climax, haven't we?' said Kangetsu, twirling the cord of his haori overcoat between his fingers.

'. . . and I saw, when I arrived there, someone *else* had come, and was hanging from the very same branch I'd been studying earlier. "*You . . . only by a whisker,*" I said to the corpse, "*. . . have done something regrettable.*" The more I think about it, whichever way you look at it, I was at that time wholly possessed by the God of Death. If someone like William James or the like were to hear all this, I wonder if he might posit that the realm of death, of the subconscious, and the real-life world I exist in, had all interacted with one another through some kind of causal connection. Nonetheless, a truly uncanny event took place,' said Meitei soberly.

The master, while believing himself to have been taken for a ride once again, said nothing but responded by stuffing his cheeks with mochi rice cakes filled with red bean paste, and chewing on it all the while making a *mogu mogu* sound.

Kangetsu carefully raked over the ash in the brazier, sniggering with his eyes downcast, but before long he opened his mouth to speak. He continued in an exceedingly subdued tone.

'There may well be some who'd listen to your strange tale and would have trouble believing it. But not I, for I *also* had a similar experience recently.'

'Oh, so you wanted to hang yourself, too?'

'No, no, my story doesn't involve necks. But, thinking about it now, my experience also took place at the end of last year, and on the *exact* same day and at the same hour as yours, Sensei.'

'That *is* interesting,' said Meitei, also stuffing his face with a particularly large piece of red bean paste-filled mochi.

'On that day, I found myself double-booked – a New Year's party at a friend's house in Mukojima, and also a recital, happening on the same evening and in the same place – and so I took my violin along with me. It was a successful meeting with some fifteen or sixteen daughters and wives in attendance, and everything was prepared delightfully. After the dinner and performances we all lost ourselves in conversation and before long it had grown quite late. I was about to make my excuses, say my goodbyes and head home, when the wife of a certain professor came to sit beside me and asked me in a low voice if I had heard anything about a certain girl's recent illness. As a matter of fact, I'd run into the girl in question some two or three days prior, and she'd seemed perfectly fine then. But I was further shocked to hear more details of the circumstances surrounding her illness – that she'd fallen ill suddenly, the very same evening of the day I'd met her; how she'd talked incessantly in a state of delirium without pause, and had blurted out many surprising things. None of this would have been out of the ordinary, but apparently she had blurted out *my name* a number of times during her state of delirium.'

The master was of course silent, and even Meitei-sensei refrained from saying anything hackneyed like, 'Lucky you!' They both listened attentively in silence.

'When they called for a doctor, he was unsure of the diagnosis, but in any case the girl in question had a raging fever and there was a concern that the illness might already be attacking the brain. If the sleeping pills he had administered did not ease her symptoms, her case might take a turn for the worse; as soon as I heard his prognosis I feared the worst. I felt as though I were in a nightmare in which the air around me had solidified, and it seemed as though it were closing in on all sides, suffocating me. On the way home, this was all I could think about, and it pained me deeply. How beautiful she was, how cheerful, how sound in body the girl in question had been when –'

'Just a minute. I don't mean to be rude, but you've all the while been referring to this young lady as *the girl in question*, not just once, but a few times since you began your story. It seems like a hindrance to the narrative, so how about just telling us her name, eh?' said Meitei, looking to the master for his support, who gave a reluctant, 'Hmm . . .' in response.

'Ah, but that would compromise the privacy of the girl in question, so whilst I appreciate your concern, I must respectfully decline your kind proposition.'

'Ah, I see now – you plan on leading us up the garden path with vagueness, I see, I see, please continue.'

'No quips, or witticisms, if you please. This is a story of an extremely *grave* nature . . . Anyhow, the more and more I thought about how suddenly the girl in question had been taken ill, the more I thought deeply about the scattering of blossoms and the falling of the leaves, and I was gripped by profound feelings about the fleeting impermanence of all worldly things. It was as though I'd been struck abruptly by a deep depression and every ounce of energy and vigour had left my entire body in an instant. And it was in that staggering and faltering manner that I came to find myself on the Azumabashi Bridge. I approached the guardrail and looked down, unsure if it was high or low tide; I saw only the black waters undulating below. A lone rickshaw came from the direction of

Hanakawado and passed by me over the bridge. I watched its lantern burn, gradually fading, becoming smaller and smaller until it disappeared entirely at the Sapporo Beer brewery. I looked down at the waters again. And when I did, I heard a voice coming from further upstream in the distance, calling my name. *Who on earth could be calling out to me at this hour?* I wondered and looked out over the water's surface, but could discern nothing in the darkness. I must've imagined it, and hastened to go home, but I had only gone two or three paces before, once more, I heard the same voice calling me faintly from far away. I froze, once again, stood stock-still and strained my ears to listen. The third time my name was called out, I had to grasp the guardrail to steady myself, for my knees were trembling in fear. I couldn't tell whether the voice came from far away, or from the bottom of the river bed itself, but one thing was certain — it was the voice of the girl in question.

'Without thinking, I replied to her, "*Yes!*" My reply was louder than I expected and echoed over the peaceful waters. I was taken aback by the sound of my own voice, and looked about me in surprise. I couldn't see anyone or anything, neither man nor beast, not even the moon. I was wrapped up in a cloak of midnight, and suddenly it became irresistible — all I wanted to do was follow the voice of the girl, to the very place from whence it came. The voice of the girl in question, once again sounding as though she were in pain, pierced my ears, pleading, begging for help, and so this time I answered, "*I'm coming now!*" and I climbed up on to the guardrail, and gazed down into the black waters. As I watched the flowing current I firmly resolved that if she called me again, just once more, that this time I would dive in, and sure enough, once again that sorrowful voice floated towards me, tugging at me like a thin piece of thread. *Now! This is it!* I thought to myself and, bracing myself, I leapt from the guardrail with all my power, immediately falling like a stone, with no regrets.'

'So you really jumped?' asked the master, blinking his eyes in shock.

'I never thought you'd go that far,' said Meitei, pinching the tip of his nose.

'After I leapt, I lost consciousness, and for a time everything felt like a dream. After a while, I opened my eyes to feel a coldness seeping into me, but I felt no patches of wetness anywhere on my body or clothes, and it didn't feel like I'd swallowed any water either. Yet I knew for certain that I had jumped . . . it was all quite odd. I was wondering at the strangeness of everything, when I realized what had happened. And I was most shocked. Of course, I'd *meant* to jump into the water, but somehow I'd made a mistake and jumped in the completely wrong direction – I'd jumped *backwards*, into the middle of the bridge, which was truly rather disappointing. And now, because I'd foolishly confused forwards and backwards, I would never be able to follow that mysterious voice to the place from whence it came.' Kangetsu grinned to himself while, as ever, fiddling about with the string of his haori overcoat.

'*Ha ha ha*, very funny! And how peculiar that you had such a similar experience to my own. As I said before, this would all make great material for Professor James, don't you think? If one were to write an illustrated book on the subject of the divine response in humans, I imagine it would cause quite a stir in the literary world . . . and what became of the girl in question?' asked Meitei-sensei, persisting in his enquiry.

'When I paid a New Year's call on her family some two or three days ago, I saw her at the gateway playing badminton with the maid, so it seems she's made a full recovery from her illness.'

The master, who had been quietly meditative for some time, at that point finally opened his mouth to speak.

'I, too, experienced something,' he said, not wanting to admit defeat to the other two.

'Experienced *something*? What on earth could *you* have experienced?' Meitei looked down his nose at the master.

'My experience also happened at the end of last year.'

'What a coincidence that all of our strange experiences happened at the end of last year,' said Kangetsu, laughing. A piece of mochi was stuck in the gap of his broken front tooth.

'And I suppose it was on the same day at the same hour,' said Meitei, butting in jeeringly.

'No. It was a different day, perhaps around the twentieth. My wife, in lieu of an end-of-year gift, had asked me to take her to see Settsu Daijo perform a storytelling at the puppet theatre as a treat. When I asked her which story he would be performing, my wife checked the newspaper and told me it would be *Eel Valley*. I told her I wasn't a fan of *Eel Valley* and could we perhaps go a different day to see something else? The next day, she came to me with the newspaper and said that today it was *Horikawa*, and wouldn't it be good to go see that one? "*Horikawa* is mainly a lively shamisen performance, and while the music is great it lacks substance as a story," I said, "so could we perhaps skip that one, too?" My wife pulled a decidedly discontented expression, but withdrew from my study, nonetheless.

'The day after, she came and told me that the performance for that day was *The Temple of Sanjusangendo*, and that come what may, she wanted to hear Settsu Daijo perform this particular story. "It may very well be that *The Temple of Sanjusangendo* is not to your liking," she concurred pressingly, "however, you're taking me to hear what I want as a treat, so let's go." "If you want to go so badly," I said, "then I'm more than happy to take you. But if, as you say, it really is a once-in-a-lifetime performance, I'd wager it'll be a full house, and we can't exactly expect to get a seat so easily. In any case, is it not more proper to first enter what is known as a *chaya* in order to reserve tickets ahead of time? It wouldn't be right and proper to deviate from this established protocol, so while it is such a shame, perhaps we'd better give up on the idea of going today." To which my wife responded with a terrible look in her eyes, "I may be a mere woman and have no idea about such complicated procedures, but *I* heard from both Ohara's mother *and* Suzuki Kimiyo that *they'd* been able to see a wonderful performance without following any of this *proper protocol* of which you speak. Now you may well be a teacher and a stickler for *protocol*, as you put it, but that doesn't mean for a second that we can't go hear a performance without all of that laborious nonsense. You really are *too* much!" she said in a wavering voice, as though she were about to sob. "If you feel that strongly about it," I said, capitulating, "then let's go. We can hop on a tram after we've eaten supper and go together." "If we're going," she said, suddenly revitalized, "we need to arrive there by four p.m. sharp. No time for your dawdling, dilly-dallying or lollygagging!" "Why must we be there for four?" I asked in return. "Because," she said, "I also heard from Suzuki Kimiyo that if we don't get there by four it'll sell out, and we won't be able to get in." "So, you're saying that if we don't get there by four p.m. on the dot, we won't be able to see the performance?" I double-checked. "Correct. We'll miss out on tickets," she answered. And that, my friends, was when the strange thing happened. At that precise moment the shivering chills began.'

'Your wife began to get ill?' asked Kangetsu.

'Oh, no, my wife was perfectly fine, dear lad. It was I who suffered. It was as if I were a child's balloon who'd been pricked with a pin, and all at once I felt myself shrivelling up and deflating. My eyes spun dizzily, and I could no longer move my body.'

'A sudden attack of illness!' Meitei chipped in, by way of explanation.

'Ah! How unfortunate! My wife's one wish in a whole year, which I so desperately wanted to fulfil. For all I ever do is scold her, disregard her feelings, overload her with housework, make her look after the little ones, and yet alas! I was unable to reward her for all her cleaning and kitchen work. Worse still, at this fortunate time in my life, I had four or five big notes in my bulging wallet, and time enough to take her. If she wanted to go, I wanted to be the one to take her. I wanted so desperately to take her, but with this terrible chill and dizziness, I couldn't even put on my shoes, let alone ride on a tram. *What rotten luck! Oh, what rotten luck!* I thought to myself as the chills and dizziness intensified. If I could only just get a visit from the doctor and be prescribed some medicine before four p.m., I'd be right as rain and raring to go.

'Upon discussion with my wife, we sent a messenger to call for Dr Amaki, but unfortunately the messenger came back informing us that the good doctor had been on call all night, and had still not returned from the University Hospital. But, the messenger assured us, he would be home by two p.m. at the very latest and upon his return would come straight to see me. *Oh, what rotten luck indeed!* If I were to perhaps take some medicinal apricot water now, I'd surely be better by four, but when the fates are against us, things never go to plan; so despite my noble intentions of taking pleasure in the seldom-seen joy on my wife's face, these best-laid plans had come crashing down around me. My wife looked at me with a reproachful expression. "So, you're telling me you can't *possibly* go?" she asked. "I can go! I must go! I . . . I . . . I'll do everything within my power to get better by four p.m. – you'll see! Go wash your face and change into your best kimono, wait for me, and you'll see . . ." Although I mouthed these words, I experienced a turmoil of conflicting emotion deep within my heart. The chills worsened to violent shivers, my eyes increasingly spun in their sockets. If I wasn't able to recover completely by four and keep my promise, there was no telling what this narrow-minded woman would do. It had become a decidedly miserable situation. How could I make things right?

'At that very moment it occurred to me that, should the worst happen, it might be the perfect opportunity for me to perform my duty as a husband towards his wife – to explain at length the principles behind the fleeting shifts and changes of human life, and elaborate upon the Buddhist teaching that all living things must die – and that now was the right time for me to do this, for should things continue to deteriorate, this would be my last chance. I resolved to seize the moment, and immediately called her into my study. "Darling, I've called you here, and while you are just a woman, you surely know the English proverb: *many a slip 'twixt cup and lip –*" "English?! Who the hell understands that sideways-written scribble? You know *full* well I don't know English, and you're just using it on purpose to befuddle and belittle me. Now, if you please, I don't understand English, and if you're so in love with English, well, why didn't you go ahead and take up with one of those graduates of the mission school for a wife? *Really*, I don't know anyone in this world as cold-hearted as you!" She said all this with a remarkably angry expression. And so, it seemed even my own hand slipped while bringing the cup to my lip – my plans fell to pieces.

'Now, I'll solemnly swear to you two fellows, too,

I didn't use English out of any intent to deceive. It slipped out unawares, I promise you, purely due to the genuine feelings of love I have towards my wife, and for my motives to be so misinterpreted by her put me at a loss. Moreover, by now, due to the chills and vertigo, my brain had become somewhat disordered – in my efforts to expound on the principles behind the vagaries of human life, and the Buddhist teaching that all things must pass, I had become flustered, and had completely forgotten the fact that my wife knew no English, thus I had used it without noticing. The more I thought about it, the more I realized that it was I who was in the wrong, and that it had been a complete oversight on my part. And yet, owing to this blunder, my shivers intensified even *further*! My eyes spun wildly in their sockets.

'My wife, following my instructions, went to the bathroom, stripped to her shoulders and began to put on her make-up, she then took out her best kimono from the tansu chest of drawers and began to get dressed. Having done all this, she waited with all the appearance of being able to leave at the drop of a hat. I was on tenterhooks. While I desperately hoped that Dr Amaki might come soon, when I looked at the clock it was already three o'clock. Only an hour left till four. "Shall we leave soon?" asked my wife, opening the door of my study and peering inside. You might think it a little silly to praise one's wife so, but seeing her face at that moment I have never thought her more beautiful.

Having stripped to the waist and washed herself with soap, her skin was glowing in wonderful contrast to the black silk haori overcoat she wore. That freshly cleaned face, coupled with a desire to hear Settsu Daijo, made her shine with the perfect union of the tangible and intangible. I was overcome with a feeling that I must at all costs satisfy her desires by leaving the house. *Right*, I told myself while smoking a cigarette, *I'll muster the energy somehow, and then let's go* . . . and it was at that point that Dr Amaki arrived.

'It was all going just as planned. He asked about my symptoms, inspected my tongue, took my pulse, tapped my chest, examined my back, pulled my eyelids up, massaged my cranium, and then pondered deeply for a while. "Is it fatal? How long do I have left?" I asked, to which the doctor replied calmly, "No, there doesn't appear to be anything wrong in particular . . ." "So, nothing that would prevent his leaving the house and taking a short trip?" asked my wife. "Indeed not," said the doctor, again pondering something deeply. "As long as he's feeling up to it, that is . . ." "I *do* feel rotten," I said. "In any case, there is a medicine I can prescribe." "Medicine? Gosh . . . this is all beginning to sound quite serious." "Not at all, there's no need to worry, so please don't get yourself all worked up," said the doctor before leaving. At which point it was now half past three. The maid was sent to pick up the medicine. She was under strict orders to go as fast as she could, and she did just that, returning promptly. A quarter to four. Fifteen minutes left. At about ten to four, despite not experiencing anything like this before, all of a sudden I was gripped with a violent nausea. My wife mixed the medicine in a tea cup and placed it in front of me, yet when I tried to reach out for the cup, my stomach was gripped with sharp and aggressive pains. I could do nothing but put the cup back down on the table. My wife pressed me. "The sooner you drink it, the sooner those pains will stop, won't they?" she said. If I didn't drink it quickly and get out the door, I'd be failing in my duty. I boldly grasped the cup and made to bring it to my lips, but again those spiteful pains in my stomach attacked me with a vengeance. As I grasped the cup in my trembling hand and made to bring it to my lips to drink, the clock in the tea room chimed out *ding-dong, ding-dong* – four o'clock. Four o'clock, no time for dawdling, so I grasped the cup firmly, and – oh, how marvellous! Oh, how wonderful! – at precisely the chime of four o'clock the nausea subsided, and without any hint of pain I was finally able to drink the medicine. At ten past four, I understood for the first time in my life the genius of the great Dr Amaki – the chills and dizziness I'd been experiencing before disappeared as though they'd been a dream. I was so happy to have made a complete recovery from an illness I'd thought incurable.'

'And so then you went to the theatre?' asked

Meitei, with an expression that suggested he'd like to get to the point as soon as possible.

'I wanted to go, but it had already gone four, and it was my wife's opinion that we wouldn't get a seat, unfortunately, and so we decided to call it all off. If only Dr Amaki had come fifteen minutes earlier, I might have carried out my duty and my wife would have been content. A mere fifteen minutes' difference; it truly was a shame. I still think about it now: how tiny things can have huge consequences.'

The master, having finished his tale, gave off the air of someone who had solemnly fulfilled his duty. Most likely he felt he could now hold his head up high in front of the other two.

As ever, Kangetsu revealed his broken tooth while laughing. 'What a pity!' he said.

Meitei, true to form, feigned ignorance and played dumb. 'Your darling wife really must be most happy to have such a kind and caring husband as you,' he said, almost as if speaking to himself. From the other side of the shoji sliding screen door came a muffled *ahem* – the sound of the mistress clearing her throat.

All the while, I had been sitting quietly listening to these three tell their tales, one by one, and had found them neither amusing nor moving. These creatures called 'humans', purely in order to kill time, waste it by flapping their jaws – laughing at things that aren't funny, finding interest in things that aren't interesting – and other than this, they have no discernible talents to speak of. I was already very aware of my master's selfishness and narrow-mindedness, but since he is indeed a man of few words, there was always something mysterious or ineffable about him. This tight-lipped mysteriousness even commanded a little respect from me, yet after hearing his pointless tale just now, all of that respect morphed into contempt. I wondered to myself why he couldn't just sit and listen silently to his two friends' stories, and leave it at that. How did it profit him to joke around and talk such nonsense, purely out of a desire not to lose their friendship? Was there any written record of his beloved stoic Epictetus acting in such a manner? I had no idea. But in short: the master, Kangetsu and Meitei are like happy-go-lucky hermits, like sponge-gourds blowing in the wind, and even though they maintain a detached and aloof air, they have all the same wants and desires as the rest of the world. Their hearts and minds are filled with the spirit of rivalry, and even their light-hearted banter is underlined with a clear subtext: *Win! Win! Win!* If they took it a step further, they would become just like the ordinary ignorant people they so often made fun of, and from a cat's perspective, that would really be quite a shame. Their single redeeming feature was a smattering of literary knowledge, including how to tell a half-baked story.

★

Reflecting on these three fellows and their stories, I suddenly grew quite bored, and decided I would rather take myself off to the garden entrance of the koto teacher's house to see how Miss Calico's health was doing. The New Year's pine decoration had been removed from the gate already as it was now the tenth of January, but it was a bright cloudless day, and the sun shone down from high in the azure sky, illuminating all and everything brilliantly. The surface of their small garden presented itself with more freshness and vibrancy than when it had been bathed in the first light of the New Year's dawn. There was a single zabuton cushion on the wooden veranda, but no sign of anyone at all. The shoji sliding doors were all shut tightly and I wondered whether the koto teacher had perhaps gone out to the bathhouse. It made no difference to me whether she was home or not, but I had hoped Miss Calico would be receiving visitors and feeling better – that was my only concern. It was deathly quiet and peaceful with no one around, and so I padded up on to the wooden veranda with my muddy paws, plopped myself down on the zabuton cushion and enjoyed the sensation of drowsily closing my eyes. I was just dozing off, and had inadvertently forgotten all about Miss Calico while I slept, when suddenly I heard human voices coming from the other side of the shoji sliding doors.

'Thank you for your trouble. Was it ready?' The koto teacher had not gone out after all.

'Yes, ma'am! Sorry for the delay. When I arrived at the Buddhist idol shop, the craftsman said he'd just finished making it.'

'Let's have a look, shall we? Ah! It's beautifully made . . . with this, I think Kitty-chan can finally rest in peace. The gold won't peel off, will it?'

'Oh, yes. About that, when I checked with him to make sure, he said that since he'd used nothing but the finest materials it would last better than even some of the memorial tablets he's done for humans . . . and then, look here . . . the Chinese characters he's inscribed for Kitty-chan's posthumous name *Honourable Devout Cat*, you see the kanji there – 猫誉信女 – he said he's changed the shape a little of the calligraphy to make it look more well-rounded and fashionable.'

'Well now, let's place it on the altar and light a stick of incense for her.'

Had something happened to Miss Calico? Certainly, there was something strange going on. I got up from the cushion.

Ding!

'I adore thee, oh Honourable Devout Cat! I adore thee, oh eternal Buddha, I adore thee, oh eternal Buddha,' came the sound of the koto teacher's voice chanting: *Namu Amida Butsu, Namu Amida Butsu.*

'Here, you pray now.'

Ding!

'I adore thee, oh Honourable Devout Cat! I adore thee, oh eternal Buddha, I adore thee, oh eternal Buddha.' This time it was the maid's voice chanting: *Namu Amida Butsu, Namu Amida Butsu.*

Suddenly, my heart began pounding. I stood stock-still on the zabuton cushion, my eyes unblinking, like a wooden sculpture of a cat.

'It really is awful what happened. And it all began with just a little cold.'

'If only Dr Amaki had given her some medicine, she might have fared better.'

'You're quite right, ma'am. That Amaki is a quack, he really didn't take Kitty-chan seriously enough.'

'Come now, you shouldn't talk badly about others. All life must come to an end.'

It appeared Miss Calico had also been administered to by Dr Amaki.

'When all's said and done, it was probably all the fault of that teacher's ghastly stray cat – always bothering her to come out to play. I think that's what caused it all, you know.'

'Yes, ma'am. It's all the fault of that brute.'

I wanted to offer some defence against this slander, but now was not the time, so I patiently swallowed my pride and listened. The conversation broke off for a moment before resuming.

'No one in this life is *truly* free, you know. A beautiful cat like our Kitty-chan dies far too young.

Meanwhile that ugly stray lives on to carry out his mischief . . .'

'You're exactly right, ma'am. You'd have to look high and low to find a cuter cat than our Kitty-chan. I'd say there's never been another person in the world quite like her.'

The maid referred to Miss Calico as a *person* rather than a *cat*. I suppose in the maid's mind, cats and people are all cut from the same cloth. But now I came to think about it, there was something altogether too feline about the maid's face.

'If only it had been *him* rather than Kitty-chan . . .'

'I'll bet you everything would've turned out better if that teacher's mangy stray had died instead.'

Turned out better? For whom, exactly? I've not had the pleasure of dying just yet, so can't say whether I'd like it or not, but the other day it was a little chilly and so I clambered into the pot for storing used coals, thinking I might warm up a little. Anyhow, the maid-servant had no idea I was inside and she came along and put the lid on. The pain I felt at that time was so terrifying that I can barely even think about it now. According to Mrs Shiro, had those pains continued for only a little while longer, I would now be dead. While I wouldn't complain if I had to sacrifice myself for Miss Calico, if the act of dying required *such* pain, I don't know . . . let's just say, I don't particularly *want* to die for anyone.

'However, I've no regrets, for we managed to get the priest at Gekkeiji Temple to read the sutras, even for a cat, and also to give Kitty-chan her posthumous Buddhist name.'

'Very true. That was most fortunate. Although, I must say, that priest read those sutras awfully quickly.'

'It did feel short, didn't it? But when I asked him if it wasn't too rushed, the Gekkeiji priest told me that he'd selected the most appropriate sections of the scriptures, and that it would most certainly be plenty good enough for a cat to enter the Pure Land.'

'Oh my! And meanwhile *that* blasted *stray* . . .'

Whilst it's very true, as I've said before, that I still have no name, this maidservant takes too much pleasure in continually calling me *that stray*. Quite the rude woman.

'But *that* rotten *stray's* crimes are so severe, no amount of reciting sutras will save *his* beastly soul!'

I'm not sure how many hundreds of times I was referred to as *that stray* during their conversation. I'd reached my limits with this tedious talk and gave up listening. I got up from the cushion, stepped down from the engawa wooden veranda, and gave myself a wonderful stretch before shaking out all eight thousand, eight hundred and eighty hairs on my body all at once. From then on, I never once set hide nor hair in the koto teacher's residence. I venture to say, I wouldn't be surprised if that koto teacher hasn't by now also had her own sutras recited by the priest of Gekkeiji Temple.

As of late, I don't feel bold enough to go outside. I feel weary of this world. I've become a hermit-like cat in the manner of the master. I've also come to believe now that it's not entirely out of the question that the reason why my master shuts himself away from the world, closeted in his study, is perhaps indeed owing to lost love.

Because I have still never caught a rat, the kitchen maid did at one time put forward an argument for my eviction. However, the master knows that I am no ordinary cat, and that is why I continue to while away my days lazily in the house. On that count, I do feel a deep sense of gratitude towards the master, and I never hesitate to show him great respect for his skills of perception. And so, it doesn't overly bother me that the kitchen maid continues to mistreat me. I'm sure that before very long, someone as skilled as the left-handed sculptor Hidari Jingoro from the Edo period will come along and carve a sculpture of me at a temple gate, just like Hidari's at Nikko. Or a Japanese version of the French painter Théophile Steinlen, who painted the posters for Le Chat Noir, will immortalize my visage on canvas.

When that does happen, simpletons like the kitchen maid will be ashamed at their own lack of perception.

Brief ENCOUNTERS

Short books. *Timeless stories.*

Louisa May Alcott
Behind a Mask

Margery Allingham
The Case of the Late Pig

Margaret Atwood
Significant Moments

Jane Austen
Lady Susan

J. G. Ballard
Venus Smiles

Simone de Beauvoir
Woman of Genius

Ingmar Bergman
Sunday's Children

Roberto Bolaño
Distant Star

Jorge Luis Borges
The Book of Imaginary Beings

Richard Brautigan
In Watermelon Sugar

Mikhail Bulgakov
The Fatal Eggs

Toni Cade Bambara
First Light

Italo Calvino
The Castle of Crossed Destinies

Angela Carter
A Souvenir of Japan

Vera Caspary
Laura

Eileen Chang
Young at the Time

Colette
The Cat

Arthur Conan Doyle
The Parasite

Anita Desai
Fire on the Mountain

Charles Dickens and Wilkie Collins
The Lazy Tour of Two Idle Apprentices

Fyodor Dostoevsky
A Gentle Spirit and A Faint Heart

Fumiko Enchi
Masks

F. Scott Fitzgerald
The Curious Case of Benjamin Button

Graham Greene
The Third Man

Jacqueline Harpman
We Were Forbidden

Ernest Hemingway
The Old Man and the Sea

Brief ENCOUNTERS

Short books. *Timeless stories.*

Bohumil Hrabal
Dancing Lessons for the Advanced in Age

Ngũgĩ wa Thiong'o
Fighters and Martyrs

Aldous Huxley
Ape and Essence

Georges Perec
Things

Christopher Isherwood
Sally Bowles

José Saramago
Cain

James Joyce
The Dead

Mary Shelley
The Invisible Girl

Franz Kafka
Mouse Folk

Natsume Sōseki
An Undesirable Friend

Yasunari Kawabata
The Master of Go

Gertrude Stein
Tender Buttons

Nella Larsen
Passing

Bram Stoker
Dracula's Guest

Halldór Laxness
A Parish Chronicle

Dylan Thomas
Portrait of the Artist as a Young Dog

Ursula K. Le Guin
Paradises Lost

Kurt Vonnegut
Monkey Business

H. P. Lovecraft
The Dunwich Horror

Edith Wharton
Bewitched

Herman Melville
Bartleby, the Scrivener

Virginia Woolf
Kew Gardens

Toni Morrison
Recitatif

Richard Wright
Down by the Riverside

Haruki Murakami
Pinball, 1973

Yi Mun-yol
The Poet